THE EASTON FALLS MASSACRE: BIGFOOT'S REVENGE

EASTON FALLS BOOK 1

HOLLY RAE GARCIA

RYAN PRENTICE GARCIA

Dedicated to Carl Mikel, Sr.

1

_____

S lung low on the horizon, the sun's golden rays pierced through the branches of the mountain hemlock and fir trees. The Cascade Mountains rose from the east like a sleeping giant, their rugged terrain a natural barrier between man and the wild forests of Washington. On the wind, rust-colored leaves whispered of autumn as they swirled around a young doe lapping at the edge of a small stream, her hooves squelching in the soft mud of the bank. Birds flew overhead, cawing to one another as the trees danced in the breeze. A fresh burst of wind brought with it an unfamiliar, earthy scent. The doe's nostrils flared at the offending odor and she raised her head, twitching her ears. Wide eyes scanned the forest around her, but the cause of the scent stayed hidden, biding its time.

The doe turned warily back to the stream, every muscle tight and twitching beneath her fawn coat.

Kellen Tsosie crouched in the thick underbrush twenty yards away from the thirsty animal and tried to ignore the thorns scratching his legs. There had been rumors around town of strange sightings in the area, but the reports were inconsistent. Some said the thing had to be the biggest grizzly they had ever seen, others swore it looked like a gorilla, forgetting that the Pacific Northwest had never been home to any gorillas. Others swore it was the Dzunukwa, from the legends of the Kwakiutl tribe. Some called it "Bigfoot", or "Sasquatch". Kellen had hoped the sightings were none of those things, but couldn't deny what was right in front of him. An ancient creature who knew their kind wasn't allowed to be so close to the stream. Forbidden, even, to leave the foothills at all. Yet there it was in front of him, shattering a centuries-old alliance between Tsosie elders and the Bigfoot clan.

When his father died the year before at the age of ninety-three, Kellen became the sole keeper of that alliance. A job that, until then, had been mostly unremarkable. When he first heard of the slaughtered cattle and missing pets from the ranches on the edge of the invisible boundaries, he thought it was a grizzly. Hoped, really. Sometimes they went rogue or rabid, though rarely. But standing in front of him was no rabid bear, and Kellen could no longer deny what was happening. A Bigfoot openly rebelling against the alliance. Kellen hoped it was just one, and not the entire tribe. In awe, he stared at the massive creature in front of him. He'd only seen pencil drawings by his great-great-grandfather. No one had been face-to-face with one of them in decades because of the alliance, understood and passed down by generations of Tsosies. An alliance breaking right in front of him.

Large brown eyes peered out from behind the base of a black cottonwood tree, fixed on the doe who had settled into the damp moss at the edge of the stream. All signs of danger drifted away on the early autumn breeze. Her eyes fluttered then closed as she fell asleep. Kellen held his breath, hoping the Bigfoot would forfeit the easy meal and return to the mountains. Instead, the creature emerged from its hiding place and crept toward the sleeping doe. The large fur-covered feet barely made a sound as it covered the distance between them in seconds.

The wind picked up again and the doe jumped from her resting spot, nostrils flaring and eyes wide. She stared at the beast for a brief second before turning to leap across the small stream and back toward the safety of the underbrush, but she was too late. As her front hooves splashed into the water, two powerful arms grabbed her from behind and lifted her high into the air. The bewildered doe lurched and twisted, trying to escape the painful grasp. Hooves beat out a rhythm against the enormous beast's body and the doe's frantic bleats pierced the distance between them and Kellen.

Tears wove their way down Kellen's rugged face, twisting and curving around the deep lines. A branch cracked as he stood from his hiding spot, drawing the creature's focus away from the struggling doe. Man and beast locked eyes across the water. Kellen took a deep breath and willed his hands to stop shaking. He shook his head, staring at the Bigfoot. It remained frozen, defiantly keeping its arms wrapped around the deer. Kellen watched as the animal pulled the doe to its chest and, with a massive arm, reached toward the doe's neck and twisted. She stopped flailing and hung limp in the arms of the beast.

Kellen turned from the stream and began the long walk back through the forest, his heart aching and heavy.

2

Henry Miller and Kate Johnson were inseparable. That is, until Henry joined the United States Army. That had caused their first *real* fight, the down and dirty kind where both people said the hurtful things, the ones you couldn't take back. He loved her, he did. He loved her more than he'd ever loved anyone else besides his parents, but serving his country was all he'd ever wanted. It was something he needed to do, and if she couldn't understand that about him, then maybe she didn't know him at all. That was the last thing he had said to her as he stormed out of her parent's house that night.

He shipped out the next morning for basic training with only his mom to see him away at the airport. He waited longer than he should have, hoping Kate would show up. He found out later that she did, but had stayed out of sight behind a stack of cheap paperback books. She said she never knew why she didn't show herself, but had stood there and watched his plane leave the runway, tears streaming down her face. Before that fight, he promised her he'd stay in touch and they did for a while. It's easy to pretend you didn't mean what you said when you're miles away. It's easy to forgive and forget, push those things back to deal with another day.

When Henry wasn't training, he was cleaning. He felt like a janitor until his deployment to Iraq. But there was a lesson in there somewhere, he was told. When the other, non-janitorial training finally paid off in Fallujah, Iraq, he saw things a lot more clearly. Henry spent thirteen months in Iraq the first time, and experienced more death and gore than he had ever seen in any movie. IEDs continuously blocked routes, killing soldiers after they drove over a perfectly placed shredded burlap sack on a dirt road. Concealed as trash, it would hide a pressure plate and an explosive with a few pounds of nuts and bolts for maximum damage. When the convoys rolled by, the explosion would be followed up with small arms fire from AK47s by extremists dressed in civilian attire. Blending in with everyday townspeople, you never knew who the enemy was until they started shooting. That kind of stress was hard to deal with, constantly assessing those around you and looking for signs they weren't what they seemed. Writing to Kate was the last thing on his mind after dealing with that level of chaos on a daily basis. Even when word arrived that his dad had suffered a heart attack and Henry knew he wouldn't be able to get home in time for the funeral. Even when the devil danced among them, claiming life after life of his friends. He couldn't talk to her about any of that, didn't know how. The letters between them slowed, just small talk and nothingness until they eventually trickled to a halt. Ten years was a long time to wait for someone. That's a lot of frigid winters without another body to warm you up. He told her he understood if she moved on, but that had hurt her feelings and he had to do a little damage control. Of course, he loved her. Of course, he wanted to spend his life with her. But he needed to be *there*, for who knew how long. He thought forever, but life seemed to have other plans for him. Plans that included roadside bombs, convoys ripped to shreds, and seeing his friends torn apart.

One scorching-hot day during an escort, there had been no debris on the road, no sign of anything out of place. But somehow, one-minute Henry was in the gunner's turret of the Humvee behind a large metal shield and the next his body had catapulted four feet into the air. A brutal combination of dust and flames flooded his line of sight. Gasping for breath, his lungs filled with burning debris and chemicals, causing breathing issues he would deal with for the rest of his life. Falling back onto the Humvee, his head had struck the shield, tearing a gash above his right eye. Crates of gear stored at the rear of the Humvee shot forward, slamming into the back of his legs. The impact blurred his vision and blood flowed into his eyes from the wound on his face. He scanned the area for the enemy, but no one fired at their group. He considered himself lucky that day. They had buried the IED too deep into the ground, preventing it from inflicting the maximum amount of damage it was designed for.

Henry struggled with that for a few years: that he had survived, but six of his friends lost their lives on that same deployment. Why wasn't he killed that day? Or a hundred days before that? Why were they? He hadn't had a good night's sleep since then, and when he *did* sleep, he felt like he was betraying the memory of his fallen brothers and sisters. No one ever wanted a medical discharge, but they didn't have light duty and couldn't use him in their fight anymore, so the Army shipped him to Fort Bragg, North Carolina. There he endured a full year of medical screenings, psychological tests, and ridiculous amounts of paper-work - only to receive a disability rating, a 'thank you for your service', and a shove out the door of American Military order and into the world of civilian chaos.

Two years passed without a letter from Kate when Henry finally arrived home in the spring of '05. He joined up with a local logging crew and spent his days working, and his nights alone. After the first thaw, he ran to town for seeds. He wanted to plant carrots that year and had hoped to get a jump on the early planting crowd. Last year they ran out of both broccoli and carrot seeds before Henry even had a chance to get to the store.

He was standing at the counter of Jensen's general store, sliding a twenty across the peeling Formica into the eager hands of a pimply-faced kid, when the small bell over the front door jingled. Henry was collecting his change when the rose and jasmine scent of perfume wafted in through the open door.

Kate.

She'd worn that scent since he first bought it for her the Christmas of '94. Henry stood there, the change still in his open hand, staring at the woman he always knew he'd spend the rest of his life with. A lot changes in ten years, especially in a small town like Easton Falls. But Kate Johnson was still that beautiful blue-eyed girl who had his heart. It was her, it would always be her.

They walked next door to the Union Grill and sat in front of untouched burgers and fries, catching up on the last few years. It was as if he had never left. Kate moved in within a month, and they were inseparable once again from that day forward. Like old times, but exponentially better than either could have ever hoped. They had their rough days like everyone else, but their bond was stronger than any bad day could be. Kate comforted him when he woke in the middle of the night screaming, covered in sweat. She helped bring him back to life, helped him want to live. Henry didn't think himself capable of those kinds of feelings again. Didn't think he deserved it, after what had happened in the war. For him, Kate was the bright, beaming light at the end of a very dark tunnel. Everything was perfect, until the day a little white stick came into the picture.

Almost a month late, Kate had a feeling something was up. Henry stopped at Jensen's on his way home from visiting his parents in town and picked up the soon-to-be-offending stick. Once home, he talked her into taking the test, then paced the hardwood floor outside the closed door of their bathroom while she peed on the small strip. Afterward, she sat on the closed toilet seat and he perched on the edge of the bathtub, both alternating between glancing at their watches and staring at the small window on the stick. Avoiding eye contact, because they had very different ideas of what a good outcome would be. She willed it to be negative, and he hoped for two pink lines.

Henry won.

Two faint pink strips shimmered into view.

"Shit," she had mumbled before throwing it into the trashcan.

"Hey, honey... it'll be okay. This is a *good* thing!" Henry followed her into the kitchen, unable to wipe the grin off his face.

Kate turned her back to him. "How can you say that?"

Hurt, Henry had paused. He knew she didn't think she was ready to be a parent but had assumed they always would have a family, eventually. "Because it's us, you and me... "

Kate jerked the refrigerator door open, looked inside, then slammed it shut again. "I'm gonna grab lunch... alone."

"What the hell, Kate? This isn't bad news! We knew we'd have a kid one day, it just came sooner than we expected. It'll be okay, babe...." Henry watched as she grabbed her purse, avoiding his eyes. "I love you."

She turned around and stared at him, tears hovering on the edge of her eyelids, threatening to spill over. "I love you, too. It's just—"

"What, is this about moving? I know you want to get out of here, but doesn't this change things? This is home, Kate! It's the perfect place to raise our baby." Henry stepped toward her and reached for her hand.

"You don't understand." She pulled away from him.

"Help me, dammit. Help me understand. Why is this such a *terrible* thing?"

"Because, Henry.... it's... this place. It's fine for *you*. You've seen the world." She threw her arms above her head, indicating the vastness of everything outside of their small town. "All I've seen is this shit town and sometimes Seattle. I love you, but I don't love this place. You know that. Nothing changes because of a baby."

Henry grabbed her arm. "*Everything* changes because of a baby, Kate."

She pushed him aside and turned toward the front door. "I'm still leaving, Henry. Nothing has changed." She shoved the front door open, letting it bang in the wind behind her as she walked to her car.

It was the only time either of them talked about her wanting to leave. After that day, they hung it up like a jacket, the thick woolen kind that itched and weighed you down. Until seven months later when it wrapped itself around them, threatening to suffocate them both.

Henry knew Kate wanted to get out of there. She'd always talked of leaving, of the two of them packing up and heading south. She had grown weary of the icy winters when her bones ached for months on end and snowstorms closed down the entire town. The white stuff would pile up at their front door, packing in until it covered every inch of the square window at the top and blocking out all the sunlight. Henry would shovel a path for their Great Dane, Jager, to run outside long enough to relieve herself and zip back into the house.

Kate would mumble, "See, even *she* hates it out here."

Henry loved Kate, he knew that much. He wanted to spend the rest of his life with her. She was the only thing in the world, besides his parents, that he had to live for. When they would lie in bed together on those lazy Sunday mornings, sweat dripping down their brow from making love, Henry's life was perfect. It didn't matter what had happened in Iraq, the things he had seen and done out of duty and self-defense. It only mattered what was happening right then, with her in his arms. She had saved him.

3

Henry had picked out the perfect engagement ring, one he knew Kate would love. Conner Anderson, Henry's best friend and Easton Falls Police Officer, was with him when he bought it. They were in Seattle for a Seahawks game, a birthday gift to Conner from Henry. The game was good, home game wins always were, and the men had enjoyed a quiet ride back, stuffed on hot dogs and twelve-dollar beer. At the intersection of Third and Park Ave, a small jewelry store caught his eye. Against Conner's protests, Henry pulled into the parking lot, promised he would only be a minute, and ran into the store while Conner stayed in the truck. A small bell tinkled when he entered and an old man looked up from his crossword and smiled. Henry picked the ring out right away. Only the third one the man had pulled from below the counter, it was exactly what he imagined Kate would have picked out for herself if she had been with him. When he turned it over in his hand, he could almost hear her admonishing him for spending too much money, but he didn't care. It was beautiful. One carat, clear, Princess-Cut diamond, surrounded by smaller diamonds on a white gold band. It was perfect. Before that day, Henry couldn't have told you the difference between a Princess and Cushion cut diamond. After that day he still couldn't, but he knew every facet of Kate's ring.

He asked Kate to marry him on their back porch as the sun slipped behind the East Cascade Mountain Range in the distance, throwing copper and pink hues across the horizon. Dinner was her favorite meal, Chilean Sea Bass with roasted vegetables, cooked to perfection. Not by him; he had picked it up from Giovanni's Italian restaurant in town. He planned everything. What he didn't plan on was her hesitation. Those first few seconds of her staring at the ring, deciding which path she wanted to go down for the rest of her life. Forever.

A chilly wind blew down from the North, and Kate crossed her arms across her chest and shivered.

"Kate, honey, I love you." He had whispered from his kneeling position in front of her, his knees growing numb.

"I know. I just..." She raised her eyes to look at him. "What does this *mean*, Henry?"

"What do you mean, 'what does it mean'? It means I want to marry you, spend the rest of my life with you. I thought..." He blustered.

"This isn't about that, and you know it. What's next, then? We stay here, have the baby in our cozy little home in our cozy little town, forever? Because that's what this means. Forever. And we haven't even decided what we're gonna do in the next few months, much less forever. You know I don't want to stay here. I want *more* than this."

"More than... me?"

"I don't know." Her eyes widened as she realized she couldn't stuff the words back into her mouth, and she turned toward the mountains, leaned on the deck railing, and hung her head.

"What the hell do you mean, you don't know? What have we been doing for the last two years, then? Why are you even with me?" Henry's voice shook as he rose from his kneeling position on the deck in front of Kate.

Kate sighed and turned toward him. "Where would we live, Henry? Because I know you. The minute I put this ring on, it's settled. We'll live and die here. You know how I feel. I *don't* want to raise my child here."

"I think we have bigger things to worry about now, what the hell do you mean 'you don't know'?" He pleaded.

"Don't yell at me."

"I'm not—" He yelled before rubbing his hand across his forehead and taking a deep breath. "I'm not yelling. I think I deserve to know what the fuck is going on here."

"This isn't how I wanted this to go... you *have* to know that. I loved you." Kate took a step toward Henry.

"*Loved* me? What... are you leaving me right now?" He asked, his voice rising in disbelief.

"This isn't how I wanted to do it. Let's just talk about this later, when you've calmed down."

Henry glared at her, his face flushed red and his eyes pulsated. "No. You're telling me what the fuck is going on. Right fucking now. I deserve that much at least."

"Okay, right *fucking* now? Fine. Let's do this, then." Kate took a deep breath. "Otis isn't your son. And I'm sorry—"

"What. The. Fuck. Do you mean. He isn't mine?" Henry glanced down at Kate's swollen belly.

"It just happened. The weekend I was in Seattle for the convention. I swear, I didn't know he'd be there. We didn't plan it, it just happened. You hadn't touched me in months—"

Fire blazed from Henry's eyes as he slowly stepped away from Kate, putting distance between them. "Who?"

"I don't want to tell you right now. Maybe once you've calmed down."

He knew he'd lost the fight, without ever realizing there had been a battle. It didn't really matter who, or why. Everything he had built his world around had gone away. He couldn't be with someone who didn't love him, and he definitely wouldn't raise another man's baby with someone he didn't trust. Regardless of what the next few minutes revealed, he knew they were over. And that was harder than anything he had ever gone through, losing the one person who meant everything to him.

Henry stuffed the ring back into his pocket and stormed into their house. He watched her through the kitchen window as she stared at the mountains in the distance, wiping away tears.

That's when he realized he needed to go hunting. He had hoped one day she'd join him, that maybe then she'd see the beauty of the place. It wasn't in the small town, the rickety general store, or the small-minded people that tended to come with a place like that. The beauty was in the woods, the way the trees swayed when the wind flew in from the coast. The birds flying overhead, calling out to each other. The wildflowers blooming around your feet. Pitch-black nights filled with bright stars, the view unobstructed by city lights or smog. The quiet. You couldn't get quiet like that in the big cities, in the places Kate wanted to go to. If that was even true anymore. He didn't know what to believe.

But that was before she ripped his world away from him. His fists clenched at his sides and his heart was racing. She had not only cheated on him but had let him think the baby was his, let him think he would be a father. They even painted the nursery mint green, for fuck's sake! What was she going to do, tell him on the way home from the hospital? When Otis turned eighteen? Never tell him at all?

Henry moved to his office and sat in the worn leather chair, listening as Kate pulled clothes from hangers in the closet and rummaged through her toiletries in their bathroom. Her footsteps echoed in the hallway, pausing at the door to his office before continuing to the front door and away from the life he thought they had planned together.

When he was sure she was gone, he gathered his hunting gear and spent the rest of the night packing up his old Chevy. Halfway to his truck with his rifle in his hands, it struck him.

She was gone.

He dropped the gun case onto the ground and fell to his knees, crying out into the frigid night.

4

He set out early the next morning just before the sun came up, blasting *Alice in Chains* and *Five Finger Death Punch* from his truck radio in a poor attempt to drown out thoughts of Kate, and the child that would never be his. After about three hours, Henry pulled up to a small clearing at the edge of the Black Forest. In the middle of the clearing sat a weather-worn log cabin with a wide porch wrapping around the front of the house. Smoke curled from the chimney and the scent of bacon and coffee permeated the air around him. One of the oldest homes in the area, it had been converted to a hunting lodge by Pete Stewart and his wife, Dottie. Three rooms held two bunk-beds each, and each one had its own washroom. During the hunting season, they could accommodate twelve bodies. Lodging included a hot breakfast and dinner, but hunters had to provide their lunches.

"Hey, Pete."

Pete Stewart sat in a wooden rocking chair on the front porch, wrapped in a thick flannel jacket and holding a cup of coffee in one hand and a cigarette in the other. A ball cap hid what little he had left of his gray hair and dirt, oil, and god knew what else stained the front of his overalls.

"Hey-o Henry, what's got you out here today? You joinin' the Williams crew for that bear hunt? Sit a while, have some coffee. Dottie's got two kettles stayin' hot." Pete pulled himself up from his rocking chair with a grunt to shake Henry's hand, then plopped back down onto the seat. The old wooden slats creaked and moaned as they had for the last twenty years. "Kate pop that baby out yet?"

Henry hesitated before answering. "Nah, we still have about a week. And you couldn't pay me enough to hunt with Robert Williams. That guy's a fucking idiot. I'm going solo today. Just need to get out here for a bit, you know?" He leaned back against the porch railing and avoided Pete's gaze. The old man always knew when something was up, like a sixth sense, and Henry wasn't ready to talk.

Pete chuckled. "Yeah, you ain't wrong about Robert." He lit another cigarette. "Anythin' you wanna talk about?"

"I'm all right," Henry answered before looking around the front yard. "Where's Lucy?"

Lucy, Pete's black Labrador, had been abandoned by a hunting party about five years prior. Pete had noted the name of the men and refused to rent to them again. Since then, she'd grown attached to Pete and Dottie, and them to her. She usually lounged on the front porch with Pete, eager to greet newcomers or say goodbye to those heading out.

"You know, it's the damnedest thing. I ain't seen hide nor hair of 'er since yesterday. She was walkin' with me to check some traps. You know the ones I got over by the gully? And she stopped like she smelled somethin', then took off toward the foothills. I called her for a while but figured she'd head on home when she was done messin' around. Like she usually does, you know?" Pete stared off into the forest at the edge of the clearing. "But I ain't seen her since. I'm startin' to get worried."

"Ah, I'm sure she'll show up, she's a good one. And smart."

"Yeah, you're probably right. Well, if I can't talk you into a coffee, go on and holler at me if you end up gettin' anythin'. I'll meet you with the ATV and we'll haul her in. I got nothin' goin' today."

Henry straightened up. "'Preciate that. Good to see ya, Pete. Don't let Dottie catch you smoking." He forced a smile before turning back down the steps.

"Shhh, she'll hear you!" Pete's head swiveled for any sign of his wife. Dottie had harped on him for the past thirty years to quit smoking and while she knew he still indulged, he'd rather avoid the harsh glares and snappy comments a cigarette in his fingers would bring about. "Well, you be careful out there. Word is there's a rabid bear on the loose. Cotton's horses got all torn up."

"You know as well as I do, that Cotton's been letting his herd roam way too close to those foothills. He's just asking for trouble, there's all sorts of shit way out there. Could be a bear, could be a cougar, there's no telling. But I'll keep a lookout, thanks."

Henry walked back to his truck, the grin fading as soon as his back turned. Pete wasn't buying Henry's facade, but he still appreciated that Pete always knew when to stay out of other folks' business. That was part of the reason Henry liked him so much.

He pulled on his backpack, slung his .338 bolt-action Lapua rifle over his shoulder, and holstered the 9mm Beretta at his hip. One last wave in Pete's direction and he set out on foot toward the Cascade Mountains. A trail led from the edge of the clearing deep into the forest, wide enough for three or four men to walk side-by-side. He planned to head to the southern canyon; he'd heard a few bears were living over that way, and it would keep him far enough away from the foothills. Not that it scared him, but growing up he'd heard too many stories of the strange things beyond them. His grandmother would read him stories of the Bakwas, a small green skeletal spirit that haunted the forests surrounding the foothills of Mt. Jarvis. Legend had it that the Bakwas would wander around looking for spirits to drag into the underworld. With a long crooked nose and bony arms, he'd snag little boys and girls who had gone too deep into the woods. Henry always said he wasn't afraid of a little green man, but he still stayed close to his dad and grandpa on their hunting trips. The one that *really* frightened him, the one that kept him up at night, was the Dzunukwa. Some native tribes called them Bigfoot. Tall, covered with fur, and with a voracious appetite, the story was that they stayed on their side of the mountains as long as the humans did the same. Henry knew they were silly legends, meant to keep kids from straying too far, but it never hurt to stay on the right side of the path.

Especially if there was a rogue bear around.

And that's where Henry stayed, as the sun climbed behind him until it shone directly overhead. Fall in Washington could be the most beautiful thing in the world. Out of all the places he'd been, in and out of the Army, it was always home. The crisp, frigid air blew around him as he walked. Sometimes he could smell the ocean if the gusts were strong enough to carry over the mountains, or wafts of smoke from chimneys lighting up for the first time after a warm summer. Birds flew overhead calling to each other, and squirrels jumped from branch to branch of the fir and hemlock trees high above him. The forest floor was still green and only a few leaves had fallen from the branches, so he made his way down the path without a sound. He still couldn't understand how Kate couldn't love the place, and he thought back over the fight the night before.

Eight months before, when a little white stick turned his world upside down, he had been over the moon. He loved Kate, and couldn't imagine a better future than one with her and their child in it. They had painted the nursery even before they found out they were having a boy. Kate said the green walls would work regardless of gender, and she wanted to do it before she was too big to get around later in the pregnancy. While waiting for the first coat to dry, they had a lunch of cold pizza and danced to Van Morrison's 'Crazy Love'. Henry wasn't the most sentimental of men, but as he stood there holding Kate, smelling of garlic bread and paint and feeling her growing belly press up against him as they swayed, life seemed perfect. *They* were perfect.

But, to do that, to go for eight months letting him think the baby was his... even letting Henry pick the name Otis after his grandfather, was too much. He still loved Kate, you couldn't turn a switch on something like that overnight, but when he thought of Otis, of all the things he had imagined them doing, a knot twisted in his stomach and his heart seemed too heavy to stay in his chest. She would leave. Taking Otis, she would pack up the nursery and move away. If she even kept the name 'Otis'. He could only assume she would go to that mystery man who had stolen Henry's family. Not that it had ever, really, been his family. It was only an idea, on loan to him. The minute Kate found out she was pregnant, she had ceased to be Henry's girl. And the baby was *never* his. Henry seemed to be the outsider in the equation. He didn't know if it was better or worse to know who the man was. If given enough time alone with him, Henry couldn't be certain he wouldn't kill the asshole.

He imagined the little boy he'd never know, with Kate's curly brown hair and blue eyes. Late-night feedings and diaper changes, all the hard work that goes into a child, but also the giggles and hugs. All of it torn from him.

Henry was still lost in his thoughts when he stumbled over a large rock wedged in the ground. After getting to his feet and brushing off his knees, he looked around him. The footpath was gone and, in its place, a wild forest of tall fir trees surrounded him. He must have left the path miles before. He didn't know exactly how far out he had come. But he was far. Further than he had any right to be, or ever wanted to be. His breath quickened as he looked up in awe at the Cascades, their snow-capped tips kissing the sky. He had never been that close to the mountains in his entire life; his grandmother would be turning in her grave if she could see him. He turned around and headed toward what he thought should be the way back.

Twigs snapped and leaves rustled off to his left. Henry eased the rifle from his shoulder and clicked the safety off, leaving it ready in his hands as he scanned the surrounding forest.

"Dzunukwa are not real. Bigfoot are not real. Bakwas are not real..." He muttered to himself as he tried to control his breathing. It was ridiculous, he knew, to be so afraid of something that wasn't real, after facing very real horrors in the war. Real people, real blood, real loss. Not fairy tales or silly stories.

A stream ran between him and the foothills, fed on ice-cold water from the mountain. On the other side of the stream, about a hundred yards from where Henry stood, a dark shape lurked in the shadows of a giant hemlock tree.

Henry narrowed his eyes, but the shadows blurred into unrecognizable shapes. Impossible to see anything from that distance, he raised the rifle to his shoulder and peered through the scope.

A grizzly, and one of the biggest he'd ever seen. The thing had to be at least eight feet tall. The bear stood with its back to him. He could make out a wide torso with dense chestnut hair rustling in the light breeze. Henry calculated the distance and wondered how hard it would be to bring a full-sized bear back with him. He hadn't planned on doing anything more than clearing his head. Shooting a bear was the furthest thing on his mind. But he couldn't pass up an opportunity like that, and Pete did say he would help. It wouldn't be easy, but he had to at least try. He let the adrenaline coursing through his veins make the ultimate decision.

Henry took a deep breath, exhaled slowly, and squeezed the trigger.

The shot echoed through the forest, piercing the quiet that Henry had come for. Birds sprang from their perches and darted into the air while smaller creatures, previously hidden, scattered away through the underbrush into the safety of the shadows. Henry's heart jumped from his chest into his throat as he watched the animal drop, his eye unblinking as it stayed pressed against the scope. The animal was down; it was a clean shot.

For a moment, Henry forgot about Kate and the not-his child she carried. He didn't think about an empty nursery or how he would break the news to his mom that she would no longer be a grandmother. He hoisted the rifle across his back and jogged the short distance to the edge of the stream. The bear lay in the soft mud at the edge of the water on the other side. Henry's mouth watered at the thought of bear stew, and his toes curled in anticipation of a soft bear-skin rug beneath them. He and Kate could light a fire and recline on the floor like they used to, pour some wine, and make love until the fire died to sparkling embers in front of them.

The reality of his situation came rushing back like a boomerang, hitting him in the stomach. Henry shook his head. They wouldn't curl up on a rug, and it would be a long while before he felt a woman's touch again. He'd give the rug to his mom and invite her and Conner over for the stew. They could throw back a few beers and *not* talk about Kate or the baby, or whatever his future looked like without them.

Henry stepped into the stream. The frigid water sucked his breath away as it lapped at his shins. He walked into the water while it inched up, reaching his chest at the halfway point in the stream. He held his rifle high above him, unconcerned about his waterproof backpack. The wet stream bottom squelched beneath his feet, and fish bumped into his legs as they swam south. Shivering, he crossed to the other side and walked onto the muddy bank. Henry aimed his rifle at the creature as he walked toward it, his heartbeat quickening. It didn't look like any bear he had ever seen. Thick ruddy hair swayed as the animal's chest rose and fell in shallow breaths. It had fallen on a blanket of leaves and mud and would have looked to be sleeping if it weren't splayed into such an unnatural position. Enormous, it was larger than any bear that roamed those woods. Henry himself stood at 6'3", and the creature dwarfed him. If it had been standing, he would have been eye to eye with its bellybutton, if there was such a thing hiding amongst the dense fur.

A putrid stench emanated from where it lay, causing Henry's morning coffee to rise from his stomach and tickle the back of his throat. He eased closer to the heaving creature. Moving the neckline of his shirt over his nose, he held it there as he continued to examine the strange thing. The hind legs were longer than he expected, one twisted upward and trapped beneath the broad torso. The front legs seemed much the same, but longer and more slender than any bear's would be. Protruding from the ends of each sat smooth tan palms leading to five slender digits, similar to his own. Henry had never seen a bear like that before.

His eyes trailed back up the animal's front legs, returning to the massive heaving chest. The same deep auburn hair that enveloped the rest of the body also covered a wide muscular neck. The chin was strong and squared, and lips almost like those of a primate's peeked out through a tangle of hair a shade lighter than the rest. The animal's eyes, hazel with flecks of gold, blinked and stared at Henry before releasing tears that tracked down the side of its face and fell onto the dense forest floor beneath it. The smooth and broad nose flared with each breath in an attempt to take in more oxygen than its dying body would allow. Steam shot from the animal's mouth in short bursts as it gasped for air. Henry brought the rifle up again, determined to end the creature's suffering. The afternoon sunlight pierced through the thick canopy of trees and glinted off the barrel. The animal's eyes widened in fear as Henry approached. With shaking hands, he stopped just short of the thing and took a deep breath. He aimed the rifle at the broad chest and exhaled as he pulled the trigger one last time. Smoke curled from the hole, weaving around blood-saturated fur and ragged skin.

5

Henry eased into the mud and stared at the creature's face. Frozen in agony, wide eyes stared out into the night at nothing and everything all at once. An awful scent wafted around the animal, unlike anything Henry had ever smelled before. With a trembling hand, he touched the broad chest in front of him. It was softer than he thought it would be, almost like silk. Warmth emanated through the thick pile of hair, but he knew it would quickly grow cold in the early autumn air.

It couldn't be the Dzunukwa or the Bakwas. Sasquatch weren't real, or Bigfoot, or the million other names people called creatures like that. It had to be a mutant, a one-off. Some sort of birth defect. Because Bigfoot did not exist. They didn't. It was a deformed bear. Henry repeated this to himself a few more times. He couldn't reconcile what he was seeing with what he knew of the world. But deformities happened all the time. Or maybe it was a new animal, some evolutionary process happening right there in the foothills. When he returned to the cabin, he'd call the game warden, David Gregory. David had been warden of those parts for about five years and would know better than anyone else, what the hell they were dealing with.

A twig snapped behind him and birds flew from the tree branches, fanning out into the air. Henry scanned the forest. Fir trees stood tall and regal in the afternoon sky, but nothing else appeared. He didn't spook easily, but something about those woods and those foothills crept under his skin and pulsated there. Whatever the animal was or wasn't, he knew he needed to get out of there, and fast. Accidentally coming too close to the foothills happened sometimes, but staying longer than he should was a different beast.

Henry stepped back from the creature and pulled out his phone to call Pete. Surprised that the thing still had any charge at all, he rang the cabin, but nothing happened. He glanced at the home screen and cursed. No service. He must have been further out than he realized.

"Shit," Henry sighed, glancing around the trees that seemed to close in on him with each passing minute.

Though not as fit as in his Army days, Henry was an imposing man who could still hold his own. Logging kept him fit enough, but it would take an Iron Man champion to drag that enormous creature just a few feet, much less through the forest and back to camp. He shouldn't have lost the trail; he was a better fieldsman than that. Cursing Kate and all her distractions, he knew he was miles off track. Besides that, he needed Pete and the ATV if he wanted to bring the creature back with him. Abandoning the carcass was out of the question. If it disappeared by the time he returned, no one would believe him. Hell, he wasn't sure he believed it himself, and it was there right in front of him.

With the phone still in his hand, he opened the camera app and pointed toward the creature. He had to walk backward several steps to get the entire body in the frame, but he knew he needed to capture the moment. He laid his rifle down next to the animal for a size comparison and took a few more pictures, then closed the phone and stuck it back into his pack.

A fish splashed into the air before falling back into the stream and swimming south.

The stream was the ticket. It had a steady current that flowed south and might bring him within range of a cell tower.

Henry shrugged his backpack off and was kneeling to unzip it when another branch cracked somewhere between him and the mountains. It seemed as if the entire forest took pause. Henry sucked in a deep breath and brought his attention back to the task at hand. He knew he was being ridiculous. There wasn't anything there, there wasn't going to be anything there, and he needed to calm the fuck down and focus.

At the foot of a large willow tree, he emptied the contents of his pack and looked for something he could use to get the creature downstream. Half the contents lay strewn around him before he came upon a spool of rope.

Another twig fell somewhere off to his right.

He shook his head. "Focus, Henry... focus."

He sawed through two sections of rope with his knife and took a deep breath before turning toward the creature. He tried to ignore the stench as he knelt at the animal's legs. Gagging, he pulled the rope around both feet and tied them together, moved up the legs, and repeated the process. Henry moved up the body, binding its arms to each side of the thick ruddy torso. A black oily film covered the palms of his hands and fingers by the time he finished. Henry brought his hands to his face and sniffed, then jerked them away, coughing and gagging. He rinsed his hands in the stream before returning to the body. Taking a few quick tugs on the ropes until he was confident they would hold, Henry returned the materials to his pack, secured the rifle to the very top, and hoisted it all onto his back.

Shivering in the late afternoon air and still damp from his trek across the stream, he wasn't in a hurry to return to the almost freezing waters. But he needed to get the hell out of there, and a better option had yet to present itself.

With a few heaves, the creature's body rolled into the stream with a splash. The current was steady, and Henry threw himself into the water after the animal and clung to its fur. He guided it downstream, keeping away from the rocks and tree roots along the banks. Henry's feet sunk into the slimy mud at the bottom. As they moved further down, he found it easier to wrap his arms around the beast, pull his legs beneath it, and ride the current south.

Fish swam around them, curious about the new visitors to their waters, and nibbled on Henry's jeans and shoes. Thankful they weren't piranha or sharks - he realized he had watched one too many horror movies. Leeches. That would be next. He'd emerge from the stream with leeches covering every inch of skin and—

But leeches were the least of his problems. His arms grew stiff, tired, and sore from hanging onto the creature. His legs, previously tucked beneath his body, now dragged the bottom of the stream bed as they floated south, kicking rocks and tree roots along the way. Trees from both sides arched overhead, meeting high above Henry.

He wasn't sure how long they had drifted, only that his hands were numb, he was soaked to the bone, and if he had to cling to the dead carcass any longer, he would let go and give the thing over to the hungry fish around him. Henry planted his feet into the soggy stream-bed and headed for the shore. By the time he pulled the heavy beast over to the bank, the sun had dipped lower in the sky and the temperature dropped into the 'not bad when you're dry but freezing when you're wet' range. Henry stood fully upright and anchored his feet against the current splashing around his waist. Shivering, he heaved the animal's head onto the bank. The water swirled around them, pushing and pulling them to go back into the stream. Henry grunted, and with one final push was able to get enough of the animal onto the bank to anchor it with one hand while he climbed out beside it. Sitting on the ground above the creature's head, he grabbed the shoulders, dug his heels into the bank on either side, and pulled. The beast inched onto the muddy bank. After a few more tugs it still wasn't completely out of the water, but it would hold until he could get help.

The sun moved behind a dark cloud and thunder rumbled in the distance. Apparently being cold, wet, and keeping company with a strange creature just wasn't enough punishment for straying from the footpath. A storm was coming.

With the cascades far behind him off to his left, Henry fished his cell phone out of the waterproof backpack. His hands shook as he checked the service. One bar. Not great, but it might do. Pete answered on the fourth ring with a grunt.

"Pete, it's me, Henry. Sorry to wake you, but... I've got a bit of a problem." Henry's teeth chattered as he panted, worn out from his journey downstream.

"What's going on? What can I do?"

"I don't... shit, I don't really know. I swear I thought it was a grizzly..."

"Did you shoot someone? Oh my god, I'm coming, where are you?" Pete asked.

"No... No. I didn't shoot a... person. Shit. Okay, I'm at the stream just northeast of the Cascades, I'll send you my coordinates. Can you bring the ATV and... I guess a tarp. And some more rope? And the trailer. This thing is big."

"Sure, but... what did you shoot?"

"That's just it, Pete. I have no fucking idea."

6

Henry pulled a thermal waterproof blanket from his pack and wrapped it around his shoulders and over his head. He leaned against the base of a large pine tree, exhausted from the journey downstream. About ten feet away in the soft ground at the stream's edge, slightly more out of the water than in, sprawled the body of the strange animal. Henry had plenty of time to inspect the creature during their swim and, after gripping the dead thing in the chilly water for what had to be the longest hour of his life, he had no desire to be near it. He leaned his head back, closed his eyes, and waited for Pete and the ATV to materialize from the forest's depths. Thunder still rumbled overhead, and a swift wind rushed through the tall conifers around him. Lightning lit up the Cascades in the distance, outlining their white, snow-topped peaks against the darkening sky. Henry shivered and brought his knees to his chest, tucking them into the blanket. The season's first cold front had also ushered in a storm. Blowing in a few days before, the weather went from a comfortable 75 degrees

Fahrenheit to a chilly 51. Typically, 51 wouldn't cause concern, but a wet 51 after a long soak in icy water, was an entirely different animal.

A storm. Perfect, because nothing about that day would be easy. Not that there was ever a good time for a storm, but sitting in the middle of nowhere with a deformed animal had to be at the bottom of that list.

Fallen leaves and small branches swirled around Henry as the wind picked up speed. Glancing at the creature, Henry didn't worry about it flying away in the wind; it must have weighed at least seven hundred pounds. Even during his peak Army days, he wouldn't have been able to move the creature any further out of the water than he already had. Your muscles could only do so much before they gave up. Laying there, its head turned toward the mountains, eyes glassy and unfocused, the animal wasn't threatening in the least. But Henry still couldn't relax.

He searched the surrounding area, squinting to see through the falling rain and darkness, hoping he wouldn't find anything menacing; especially no more creatures like the one in front of him. It couldn't have been the only one of its kind. Early fall seemed to be the time of year for grizzlies to forage and pack in the calories in anticipation of winter. Henry would continue to assume it was a deformed grizzly until someone convinced him otherwise. Those things happened all the time to humans; babies born without legs, half a brain, twisted spines, or twins conjoined at the head. Nature could be a cruel bitch. Something had happened to the massive creature, some grotesque defect or contaminated water, or... Henry stopped himself. He could surmise all he wanted about what it was or wasn't, but he would have to wait for David to take a look. Henry knew when he was in over his head.

Trees rustled in the storm and the forest echoed around him. He couldn't tell which direction the sounds came from; if the storm was the cause or... something else. The early evening came alive with noises, creaks, and clatters through the trees. He tossed his cell phone into his waterproof pack when the light rain turned to a heavy downpour. The phone itself was also supposed to be waterproof, but he didn't want to take any chances.

Henry took a deep breath and moved next to the creature. Like it or not, the body was still warmer than the tree trunk he had been leaning against, and at that moment he needed all the shelter and warmth he could find. Almost two hours later, with his head still down, he didn't see Pete's ATV approaching through the trees and into the small clearing by the stream. Yelling over the storm, Pete finally got Henry's attention.

Relieved, Henry jumped up and ran to the ATV, throwing himself into the passenger seat. What it lacked in doors, it made up for in a roof, so while the rain still pelted them from the sides, they were somewhat protected from the worst of it. Henry leaned in so Pete could hear him over the steady pounding of rain.

"It's right over there!" He pointed to the stream.

Pete's eyes followed his finger, squinting to see through the storm. Recognition dawned, then confusion. "What the..."

"That's what I've been saying," Henry answered, almost yelling, as he gestured to the trailer. "Let's load her up and get her back to the cabin where we can figure it out without all this shit coming down." He looked behind him at the trailer attached to the ATV and paused. "We're gonna need a bigger trailer."

"Look, how was I supposed to know what the hell you had up here? We'll make it work."

Henry grabbed the extra rope stored in the back of the ATV and Pete grabbed his pistol.

"Really, Pete? It's dead. I made sure of that much, at least."

"I'm not takin' any chances."

They took a deep breath before plunging back into the downpour, keeping their heads down until they were almost on top of the beast.

Pete stared, unmoving.

"Pete!" Henry yelled at his friend, but he wasn't listening, still in awe of the animal in front of him. "Pete, let's go!" Henry pulled on the creature, trying to get a hold of the rope around the heavy carcass. Rigor mortis had settled in, which made the job a little easier than before, but the animal remained heavy.

Snapping out of the shock, Pete knelt to help. "Mother of everything holy, what in the hell is that smell?"

Henry glared at him. "It could be worse. I'll tell you about my trip downstream later."

Both men were panting by the time they loaded the creature onto the trailer. Pete didn't have the same endurance as Henry and, with his advanced age, he felt the strain of the heavy work and late hour.

"You okay?" Henry yelled through the noise of the storm.

Pete waved at him in answer, still out of breath.

"Well, looks like it'll hold enough, anyway. Think it'll make it back to the camp?"

Pete answered in short bursts. "Yeah. She's fine. Let's get. The fuck. Outta here."

Easing the ATV around fallen branches and pools of mud around the forest, they headed toward the hunting lodge. Henry turned sideways in his seat to keep an eye on the creature, every bump and jolt seeming to slide it a little further down the trailer.

"What, you don't trust my knots?" Pete yelled over the rain.

"I don't trust anything right now," Henry answered.

The blue tarp covered most of the creature, wrapped in rope but for two hairy legs sticking out of the end. Past the feet, the forest pulsed and breathed with the storm. Shadows ran between trees, growing smaller as they drove away. Henry swore one of them looked like a large grizzly, but that's also what he thought when he first saw the definitely-not-a-grizzly creature that lay beneath the tarp. He leaned back in his seat, eyes squinting through the branches and leaves. Nothing but trees swaying in the storm. In the darkness, every lightning strike revealed menacing shadows, arms reaching out toward them, eyes glowing yellow. He had faced worse things in Iraq, and he would not let a few shadows spook him. Henry turned back to the front, slumped low in the seat, and closed his eyes.

He was back in Iraq, alone, kneeling behind a parked single-cab pickup truck. Small streaks of red, yellow, and blue lights flew across the night sky as if a meteor shower was traveling horizontally above his position. He could hear the pings as bullets struck objects near him. Pinned down by gunfire, he would wait for breaks in the chaos to shift and lean over the windshield, leaving most of his body shielded by the truck. Then he would fire a few rounds downrange where he believed the insurgents to be, before returning to cover. An inhuman roar echoed through the night, drowning out the sound of the battle at hand... then silence. Turning around to catch his breath and scan the area, Henry screamed as he saw a large chestnut-colored creature charging at him with arms outstretched and teeth glowing white, reflecting the tracer rounds firing above. Just as the monster grabbed him, Henry jerked his body upright and opened his eyes. Panting and covered in sweat, he struggled to catch his breath.

"Pete," he said without looking at his friend. "Step on it."

"Must have been some dream," Pete exclaimed before giving the ATV a little more gas.

"Faster than that buddy, I'm feeling a little exposed."

With a jolt forward, Pete pushed harder on the gas, sending them barreling through the woods and leaving the shadows far behind.

Darkness had fully enveloped them by the time they pulled into camp. Pete pulled the ATV up to the edge of the barn and put it in park.

"Let's put it in here, you look like the walking dead. Get some sleep. We'll deal with it in the morning." Pete unchained the large barn doors.

"I'm good. I wanna get a better look at it now that I'm thinking a little more straight."

"Now, it don't matter what it is, it's still gonna be there in the morning. And you, my friend, look like hammered dog shit. Go get some sleep."

"Yeah, I guess you're right." Henry gave in. "Fuck, I'm tired."

They backed the trailer into the barn, unhitched it from the ATV, and pulled the vehicle back out, leaving the animal wrapped in the blue tarp on the bed of the trailer sitting in the middle of the barn. Pete waved Henry on into the house as he stayed to close and lock the barn doors.

When he set out that morning, Henry hadn't planned to stay the night at the lodge. But at that moment it didn't matter if he had a toothbrush or a change of clothes, because Pete was right. Henry looked and felt like shit. Rain pelted the roof of the cabin as he stripped the soaked clothing from his body. He threw his clothes across the tall headboard to dry and collapsed onto the bed, naked. Out of routine, he pulled out his cell to call Kate or to see if he had any missed calls. Old habits died hard. Somehow, he had hoped the night before was all a nightmare and she would call him asking how the hunt had gone. But it wasn't a nightmare, and she was gone.

"Henry," Dottie Stewart called from the other side of the bedroom door before knocking on the wood paneling.

"Hey Dottie, everything ok?" Henry answered from the bed.

"Yeah, yeah. You decent?"

"Hold on," Henry pulled the covers over his body. "Come on in."

Dottie walked into the room, keeping a respectable distance between herself and Henry. "I just wanted to make sure you had something to eat. I noticed you didn't have a lunch this morning. Have you eaten anything all day?"

"You know, I didn't even think about food until just now," Henry eyed the plate in her hand. A thick slab of ham nestled next to a pile of mashed potatoes and corn. A glass of water balanced on the edge of the plate.

"I'm gonna leave it right here on the dresser. You be sure to eat it all, and if you want some more just come on downstairs." She started to go, then turned around. "But you'll have to get clothes on if you do that." Dottie winked and closed the door behind her.

Famished, Henry scarfed down the plate of food faster

than he should have, but heartburn was the last thing on his mind. He wiped his hands on the jeans hanging from the headboard and rolled over to go to sleep. As exhausted as he was, rest didn't find him easily that night. More shadows, strange creatures, and darkness filled his dreams while the storm raged outside.

7

The rusty chains on the front of the barn rattled as Robert Williams and his son, Lewis, yanked on them and shoved their squat faces into the crack. They pulled the doors open as far as the chains would allow, leaving only a few inches of viewing space. The rest of the hunting party was still inside the cabin, drinking coffee and grumbling about their collective misfortune the day before. When they returned with a kill, the hunters would pound each other's backs and congratulate each other as if they had personally solved the problem of world hunger. But that morning they were irritable and quiet. There was nothing to brag about, as the only thing they had come across worth shooting had been a bear that ran away uninjured.

"If you'd a kept your damn mouth shut, we'd a shot somethin'." Robert pushed Lewis aside to get a better view. "Then we wouldn't be here tryin' to see what someone else got." Robert jerked back from the small opening. "Jesus Christ, what is that smell?!"

Lewis kept his eyes on the chain, rattling it and looking for a weak spot.

Robert turned back to Lewis, holding his shirt over his nose, and continued berating his son, mumbling through the cotton fabric. "I mean, did you see the size-a that bear? I told you to shut the hell up but no... you had to go and keep yappin' and scarin' away everything worth anything. That bear woulda been bigger than this thing whatever's under that tarp there. You'da seen it if you was payin' attention."

Lewis sighed. "Yes, sir."

While Robert and Lewis tried to get a look at the inside of the barn and the rest of the group sulked over their coffee cups, the impact of the day before was hitting Henry. He'd already downed three cups of coffee, black since they had no creamer around the place. Dottie swore it gave Pete the runs. The creamer, not the coffee. She refused to keep any in stock. If you stayed at the lodge, you had to bring your own shit.

Henry was rinsing out his coffee cup in the kitchen when a movement from the window above the sink caught his eye. A flash of blue, a Seattle Mariner's cap. Robert's favorite team, though they'd been on a losing streak since the Houston Astros whooped them in the playoffs the year before. Robert, who at that moment was standing in front of the barn and trying to get through the chain. The half-washed cup fell into the sink with a clatter as Henry ran toward the front door. Clearing the steps with one jump, he landed on the hard concrete walkway and sprinted toward the barn.

"Hey!" He shouted.

They didn't hear him, or didn't care. Getting to the creature inside held their full attention.

"What the fuck? Can't you hear me?" Henry stood behind them and clapped his hand down onto Robert's shoulder.

They turned around. Startled, the boy's eyes were wide and scared while Robert's face grew more scarlet by the second. The elder Williams shrugged Henry's hand off his shoulder and took a step back.

"What's in the barn, Henry? What's so important to warrant this big chain and padlock? You think you're better than us or something?"

"None of your goddamn business. I don't have to tell you shit, now back the fuck up."

"Yeah? Who's gonna make me? What are you trying to hide?" Robert glared at him.

"Dad, let's just go finish breakfast," Lewis tilted his head toward the cabin.

"Shut your mouth, Lewis. You're the reason we got nothin' yesterday. Go on. Go on to the house with the other losers. I'm stayin' right here 'til Henry tells me what the hell that thing is. And I *know* it's somethin' big." His eyes sparkled. "And you're gonna let me in on it."

"Like hell, you're getting in on anything," Henry drew closer, a good two hands taller than Robert, blocking the rising sun behind him. Robert was a small man; those types usually were. The kind that always felt they needed to compensate for something; prove to the world they weren't little. That kind of insecurity could breed the nastiest of men, eager to bring others down to their level so they could finally feel equal. Not that every short man behaved that way, but just about every one of that 'type' compensated for something. Short stature, receding hairline, or disappointed wives. The kind that talked a big game but usually spent their Saturday nights with a well-worn magazine and a nearly empty tube of lotion. You could practically smell the testosterone seeping from his pores.

Robert glared at Henry, his head tilted up at an extreme

angle. The morning sun shone a halo around Henry's blond hair and into Robert's eyes. Henry stood inches from Robert's balled fists.

"Why don't you back the fuck up," Robert mumbled.

"Why don't *you* get the fuck out of here, I don't want to hurt you in front of your kid, but I will," Henry replied, not backing down. He could win that fight easily. He'd broken larger pieces of shit than Robert Williams and had the scars across his knuckles to prove it.

Robert glared up at Henry and, without breaking eye contact, muttered to Lewis, "Go on now, boy. Go on up to the house and see if you can help your mama with breakfast. See if you can do that much right, at least," his voice low and mean.

Shuffling back to the cabin, Lewis kept his head down.

Back at the barn, neither man had moved. Henry's shadow towered over Robert, but that didn't seem to bother the smaller man.

"So, what are you gonna do, big man?" Robert sneered.

Henry stared down at him.

"Nothin', that's what you're gonna do. No wonder you got your buddies killed over there, you're useless."

Henry's eyes reflected the sun, flames of gold and brown flickering across them. He squared his shoulders and tightened his muscles, barely visible as a ripple beneath his long-sleeved flannel shirt. Henry swung his arm as hard as he could, open-hand slapping Robert in the face, sending him sprawling into the dirt at their feet. He was mad at the man, but didn't want to hurt him too badly, nothing like a closed fist would do. Henry's fist flexed, itching to do more than a slap. He stepped over Robert, putting himself between the bleeding man and the barn.

"What *you're* going to do is shut your fucking mouth

about shit you don't know about." Henry's voice shook with anger. "Now, take your ass inside and don't come near me again." The chains rattled as Henry stepped back against the barn doors and folded his arms.

Robert pulled himself to his feet and shuffled toward Henry, wild with anger. His fist balled and right arm twitching, he was hungry for payback.

"Robert!" A shrill cry rang out from the front porch. Miranda Williams stood there looking like she knew she'd drawn the short stick in life, but was gonna wrangle it all together as best as she could, anyway. "Robert, Pete needs your help with the fox traps."

Robert spat on the dirt at Henry's feet, blood turning the spittle a pale pink. "This ain't over."

Henry smiled. "Go on now, we'll chat later." Though he had no intention of ever talking to Robert Williams again if he could avoid it.

When Robert turned to go inside, Henry's smile faded. He still needed to figure out what to do with the creature and knowing Robert, he'd start telling everybody about it in no time if for no other reason than to irritate Henry. The man could be a real piece of work. But he needed to think, him and Pete, about what to do with the thing. Shit, about what the thing even was. And he wasn't letting Robert Williams, of all people, be in on that process.

By the time Pete came outside, Henry was working on his second cigarette, perched on the top of the wooden fence near the barn. Pete shook his head.

"Can't just let it go, can you? You know that man is always lookin' for a reason to fight, can't you just sometimes let it go? He's an ass, but he brings in good money."

"Hell no, it's too much fun getting on his bad side," Henry chuckled.

"Son, you *stay* on his bad side, no sense tryin' to get there. What was it this time? Talkin' shit about your huntin', or your girl?" Pete leaned against the fence. "Now give me one of them cigarettes 'fore Dottie comes out here."

His girl. Well, he wouldn't have to worry about that anymore, though he cringed at the thought of Robert holding that over his head for the next few years.

"Nothing," Henry answered as he handed Pete his pack and a lighter. Pete tapped the cigarettes against his palm, packing the tobacco more out of habit than necessity.

"I tell you, we gotta figure out what to do Henry, or this thing's gonna get ahead of us." He lit a cigarette and handed the pack and lighter back to Henry. "You already got that asshole in there tellin' everbody that'll listen, that you're tryin' to hide somethin' in this barn here."

"I don't give a fuck about Robert Williams, or anyone who would take what he's got to say seriously."

"Yeah, I know. Believe me... I *know*. But we still got a problem." Pete pointed to the barn doors. "What are we gonna do with *that*?"

Henry hopped down from the top of the fence. "Well, first things first, let's get her open. Did you bring the key?"

"Well, of course. It was the first thing I grabbed when I saw that asshole out here tryin' to start shit with you. I told his wife to go fetch him for me, then I got the key out of the drawer in the kitchen. I knew he was gonna be lookin' for trouble, them Williams' never were nothin' but problems."

Pete unlocked the padlock and pulled the chain through.

Henry pulled the doors open. "Now, let's see what we-"

Confronted with the full size of the creature, both men were speechless. The evening before had been hectic, dark, and unsettling. But there, in the bright light of morning, there was no mistaking the mess they had on their hands. Not much had changed with the creature itself in the time since they had last seen it. Henry and Pete stared down at the thing, neither knowing what to do next.

"Well, I guess we could call David..." Pete trailed off, unsure if the game warden was the answer to the enormous problem laying cold and stiff in front of them. "Jesus, did it smell this bad yesterday?"

"You think it's bad now? You shoulda been the one to have your face all up in it while floating downstream." Henry shook his head at the memory. "But yeah, I thought about that. We should call David... and Conner."

The front door of the hunting lodge banged shut, followed by footsteps and excited murmurs. Henry and Pete stepped to the edge of the open doors and looked around to find Robert Williams leading a handful of men toward the barn.

"Shit," Henry glanced back at the creature, his mind racing. There was no sense in trying to hide it anymore. They weren't any closer to figuring what the thing was, and it was all gonna come out eventually, anyway. Henry moved closer to the animal, placing his hand on the tarp. Men like Robert understood very little, but touching a thing is as good as writing your name on it, everyone knew that.

"See there, I told you it was something big." Robert boasted as they entered the barn, like he was the one to shoot the creature and haul it back to the camp. He couldn't shoot his way out of a goddamn paper bag and everyone knew it.

The men crowded around the trailer bed, touching the thick fur sticking out from beneath the tarp and trying to see the rest of the animal. Most had their shirts around their mouths and noses, assaulted by the awful smells emanating from the barn.

"Now, hold on just a fucking minute," Henry's voice rose above the clamor, silencing everyone but Robert, who continued to mutter beneath his breath. Henry's blood pulsed in his ears, and he could feel his face turning red. "We're calling the game warden. We're doing this thing the right way. Back the fuck up, get your hands off it before you fuck it up, and let us handle it." Henry gestured toward the door of the barn, hoping they would get the hint.

But Robert stood among his people, who either didn't know better or didn't care about how big of an asshole he could be. And they were looking to him to see what to do next, ignoring Henry.

Robert grinned at Henry. "Or what? From where I stand, you shot something illegal. This ain't no grizzly. I'm thinkin'..." he looked around at the men. "I'm thinkin' we need to call the authorities."

"What the fuck do you think the game warden is? The tooth fairy?" Henry asked, disgusted.

Robert frowned, glancing around him and back to Henry. "Well, no shit they ain't the tooth fairy, dumbass, I'm just saying, let's call them *now*. While we can all... corroborate... your story. So you don't try nothing sneaky. In fact, we should go ahead and call the Easton Falls Times, let 'em know what you did. I think they'd be mighty interested in somethin' like this."

"Nice big word there, Robert... *corroborate*. You sure you know what that means?" Henry muttered beneath his breath, "Fucking asshole."

"What? What did you just call me?" Robert asked.

"I said you're a fucking asshole, and I don't think anyone here would argue with that."

"Look here, let's all calm down and behave. Remember, you're in *my* barn. Let's just call David," Pete interrupted, pulling the warden's info from his contacts and handing the phone to Henry.

Henry held the phone to his ear, keeping his eyes on Robert.

"Hey, David. It's Henry Miller. I'm over here at Pete and Dottie's and... well, there's something you should come take a look at. What? Yes, it's an animal, why else would I call you? Okay... okay... okay, see you then."

Henry handed the phone back to Pete and sighed. "He can't be here 'til tomorrow afternoon. He's been over in League City looking into the bear attacks. Missing livestock, that kind of shit."

"Damn, that's clear on the other side of the state," Pete said.

"Maybe they'll catch it this time... unless we already did." Henry looked down at the tarp-covered mass in front of them.

"You got lucky," mumbled Robert.

"You know, that would make sense," Pete replied, ignoring Robert. "But not sure how it got all the way over here so fast."

"Well, David can figure it out. In the meantime, he said to get it on ice."

That would be easier said than done. The thing dwarfed any freezer they had at the hunting cabin, and they had a ton of freezers. Sometimes hunters wouldn't want to haul their kills home and butcher it themselves, so they left it with Pete and Dottie to handle. It was a pretty lucrative, if not messy, side business for them. Their prices were the best in the state. Of course, they charged more if you wanted to keep the skin or skulls for mounting later. Henry had helped them out many a night when he first came back to the states, to get his mind off things. They'd sit around the kitchen with empty sausage casings, grinders, cleavers, and butcher paper, knocking beers back while cutting up the meat. They always appreciated the help and offered to pay him for his time, but Henry never took the money. It was enough to get outside his thoughts for a while and be with friends.

Unfortunately, the Stewarts had nothing capable of handling an animal the size of the creature currently residing in their barn.

"What about O'Malley? He's got that big walk-in." Pete suggested.

Distracted by the problem at hand, Henry didn't see Robert uncover one of the animal's legs. "Ooo-wee boys, look at this!"

"Goddammit, can you just get the fuck out of here?" Henry placed himself between Robert and the trailer, shoving the smaller man away in the process. There were bigger problems in his world than Robert Fucking Williams. He was like a fly buzzing around your face, irritating you and keeping you from getting the real work done.

"Got himself an illegal kill and now his balls are bigger than his brains," Robert stepped close to Henry, closer than Henry ever allowed that asshole to get without knocking his teeth out.

"Really? You want to do this again? What, one bitch-slap ain't enough for you?" He glared at Robert.

Robert glanced at Lewis standing at the back of the crowd, and the tips of his ears turned red. The other men whispered to each other, a few bold enough to laugh out loud.

Dottie, always one with perfect timing, entered the barn

and assessed the situation. "What in tarnation is goin' on in here? You boys get out, I swear to you Robert if you don't knock it off, I'm gonna ban you for the rest of the season."

She knew Robert was the problem, and she knew Henry was about to handle it in a way that might add a few new scars to his knuckles.

"Saved by a woman," Robert mumbled as he walked back toward the house, more afraid of Dottie than interested in getting back at Henry.

Henry stepped toward him, stopped by a hand on his chest from Pete. "He ain't worth it, we got bigger problems."

The other men grumbled as they left the barn and headed back into the house, leaving Henry, Dottie, and Pete alone in the barn.

"And you, Peter Roland Stewart, get this stinky thing out of here before any more trouble starts."

"For God's sake Dottie, you and them damn troubles. Nothin's gonna happen, it's nothin' but a freak, a deformed bear."

"Say what you will, but say it as you're pullin' this trailer out of my damn barn."

Henry smiled at Pete before pulling his phone back out and dialing Conner's number. The local police would probably need to know what was going on in their own backyard.

8

The only freezer large enough to house the creature sat inside O'Malley's Butcher Shop, over at the intersection of Main and Hemlock Streets. The owner, Richard O'Malley, wasn't keen on the idea at all. Henry argued with him on the phone for what felt like an hour before he agreed to house the thing temporarily, with a strong emphasis on 'temporarily'.

"Just until tomorrow! That's it! Then I don't care what you do with it, but it's leaving my shop. I got a business to run. You think people want their meat hanging next to some... *thing* you found in the woods? We don't even know if it's got viruses! You know nothing, and you just expect me to—"

"I can pay you." Henry interrupted.

O'Malley paused. "How much?"

Everything had a price. Henry had a little money saved up to take Kate over to the coast for a weekend, just the two of them. She hadn't known about the trip, Henry planned it as a surprise engagement celebration. 'Surprise, she decided not to marry you. Surprise, the baby was never yours.' Not exactly what he had in mind when he started putting the money away.

"A hundred?" Henry asked. He wasn't about to let O'Malley know how much money he had to bargain with.

"Deal," O'Malley answered. "Per day."

"Dammit, O'Malley."

"It's a wee amount, and not like you have a lot of other options here, Henry. This *is* my business we're talking about, scaring away good, paying customers. How am I supposed to feed my—"

"Fine." Henry hung up and shoved the phone back into his pocket.

Pete asked, "How much?"

"Huh?"

"How much is he charging you to keep it?"

Henry chuckled. "Yeah, you know O'Malley, all right. And too fucking much. Hundred today, and a hundred tomorrow. Hopefully, by then David'll have it wherever they usually take shit like this."

"Well, let's get it out of the barn before Dottie loses her shit. You ready?"

"Yeah, I'm gonna run upstairs and make sure I'm not leaving anything."

"Don't do it, Henry," Pete warned.

Henry feigned innocence and grinned. "Don't do what?" He patted Pete's shoulder as he walked past him toward the house. "I think we have bigger problems than Robert Williams."

"Still, try to behave, would ya?"

"Always."

Henry went into the house and upstairs to the room he had slept in the night before. After a quick once-over to make sure he wasn't leaving anything, he headed back down the stairs. In the kitchen, he lingered longer than he needed to, hoping to run into Robert Williams one more time before he left.

"Henry Miller!" Pete called a warning from the front porch.

"I'm coming... I'm coming."

Three and a half hours later, when they pulled the trailer into the parking lot of the shop, O'Malley stood outside waiting for them. Dark stains covered the front of his white apron, a result of years of throwing around hunks of meat. With crossed arms and a pissed-off stare, you could smell the hostility from a mile away. The air was cool from the storms the night before, and the parking lot's potholes were full to the brim with water. The trailer splashed into the biggest one as they came to a stop. Henry jumped down from the driver's seat and nodded at O'Malley.

"Well, come on then 'fore half the town sees you or you tear up my parking lot," O'Malley grumbled.

"Your parking lot's *been* shit," answered Henry. "That's not on us."

O'Malley peeled back a corner of the tarp. "Jesus, Mary, and Joseph..."

"Yeah, we know, let's just get him inside."

O'Malley protested, "Now wait just a minute. This isn't what we talked about."

"I didn't say it *wasn't* Bigfoot," Henry's eyes gleamed with mischief.

"Your price just went up," O'Malley stood in front of the door and crossed his arms.

"Are you fucking...fine. How much?" Henry asked.

"Another hundred. And you didn't say nothing about the smell, neither."

"Here's your fucking money," Henry pulled the cash

from his wallet and shoved it toward O'Malley. "Now can we just deal with this, please?"

"Well, let's go, gentlemen." O'Malley perked up. Money seemed to have that effect on him.

It took all three men to haul the beast indoors, still wrapped in the tarp. O'Malley and Henry grabbed the front end, one at each shoulder, and Pete grabbed the feet.

"What do you think these are, size fourteen?" Pete asked, grunting under the weight.

"Nah, twenties at least," answered Henry.

"Can you two focus? I haven't got all goddamn day," mumbled O'Malley.

Henry ignored him and paused to let his eyes adjust to the dim interior of the shop. One of the oldest shops in their small town, it wasn't anything to write home about. The same old red brick covered almost every building on the strip, but the interior had been completely renovated just a couple of years before. With clean lines, white walls, and a large stainless-steel bar running the length of the back, it was unassuming but functional. On a typical day, one could hear handsaws cutting through bones in the back room, creating a symphony of the macabre with grinding saws and vacuum sealers as backup. During the hunting season, O'Malley would hire a few teenagers from around town to help out, and they could often be found pushing slabs of meat through the thin blades of the slicer on the back counter. That was all during the normal order of business. Richard had been doing all right, ever since Pete and Dottie started running specials for veterans over at the hunting lodge. They'd host 'em, then offer to pack up the kills and bring them on over to O'Malley's for a small fee. Shit, between that and the money Richard took from them, it would have been cheaper to buy a slab of beef in the grocery store. But the customers got the thrill of the hunt, a weekend of relaxation, and a few beers. That day, O'Malley had sent the help home and posted a sign on the front door asking customers to come back in two days. The butcher shop was quiet as a graveyard, with only the copper scent of old blood in the air to keep you company.

Once inside the walk-in freezer, O'Malley made a clearing on the floor beneath the hanging torsos of three pigs, one cow, and two geese, while Pete plopped down in a chair to catch his breath. The walk-in freezer was new, installed a few months prior by a company out of Seattle. Metal surfaces reflected the bright lights from above, and silver chains hung from the ceiling. It was O'Malley's pride and joy, and he wouldn't let Henry or Pete forget about it. On the concrete floor sat more chains, still in their sealed boxes. Henry and O'Malley pushed the boxes to the side and pulled the animal into the cleared space.

"I'm getting too old for this shit," Pete pulled a pack of cigarettes from his shirt pocket. "Henry, you got a light?"

"Not in here, you don't," interrupted O'Malley as he wiped his hands on his apron. "I'm not gonna have all my meat smelling like smoke. Bad enough it's gonna smell like this giant piece of rotten ass you dumped on me. Take that shit outside."

"Maybe we should wait for David to get here... let him decide if he wants to unwrap it or not. It would be easier for him to get it out of here if it was still wrapped, right?" Henry asked.

O'Malley stopped, pocketknife poised over a short length of rope. "Bang on. That's the best damn idea you've had all day." He closed his knife with a flick of the wrist and stuck it back into his jeans. "The less I have to touch this thing, the better. It fucking reeks. We're gonna have to move everything else over to the smaller freezer in the back, don't want it catching whatever this has. If you brought some damn maggots in with it, I swear to you—"

"Dammit, O'Malley, do you think we *want* to be here? We don't, not any more than you want us to be. What the fuck choice do we have? David said to get it on ice, and this is the closest thing we got. Now, I've had a long night, and it looks to be an even longer day, so can you just shut the fuck up about it?"

The room fell silent.

"Shit, I'm sorry. It's not you. This... *thing* is just a lot to deal with. And at the worst possible time." Henry apologized.

Pete touched Henry's arm. "Everything all right there, Henry?"

"Yeah, I'll tell you about it later. Let's knock this out."

Once they moved the other meat to a different freezer, the three men hauled the creature into the walk-in space, shivering in the frigid air from the sweat on their arms and face.

"I need a drink. Pete, you coming? I'm buying."

O'Malley argued, "Oh fine, great, leave me here with this—"

Pete and Henry left O'Malley grumbling as they headed down the street.

9

Pete and Henry set off on the short walk to Lindy St. Bar and Grill. Calling it a "Grill" was a very loose interpretation of the greasy burgers and fries they served until the kitchen closed at 9:00 p.m. Locals knew to avoid the food or risk spending the night hugging the porcelain throne. The bar was first and foremost the neighborhood watering hole, ran by Walter Roman since before anyone could remember. But that's not what they came to Lindy's to do... remember. Most came to forget; their wives, their bills, and their shitty jobs.

Henry shivered as they walked down the sidewalk. "We supposed to get another storm in?"

"Yeah, should be rolling in soon. Though we might miss the bulk of it 'till tomorrow. Looks like it's hovering to the south, 'round Waller."

Henry glanced at the darkening sky above him. "Let's hope we miss it. There's bigger shit to deal with right now."

"So... you gonna tell me what's eatin' at you?" Pete asked, glancing at Henry as they walked.

"Besides fucking Bigfoot in a freezer back there?" Henry jerked his thumb behind them and managed a weak smile.

"Yeah. Besides fucking Bigfoot."

Henry sighed and looked down at his feet as they continued to walk. "So... you know how I bought that ring for Kate?"

"Yeah."

"She said no—"

"What? Why—"

"Hold on, there's more." Henry stopped on the sidewalk and turned to face his friend. "We're not getting married. We're not getting *anything*. She moved out. And," Henry paused, "Otis... the baby... isn't mine."

"Are you fucking *kidding* me?"

"Look," Henry closed his eyes for a moment and held up his hand. "I know it's a lot. But I'm tired and I just want a beer. I'll tell you all about it later, I promise. Ok?"

Pete searched Henry's face before answering, "Got it," and followed Henry the last few feet to Lindy's wooden door.

Before they had fully stepped over the threshold, all eyes inside turned toward them. Conversations dwindled and a pool ball dropped into a corner pocket with a thud as a hush fell over the crowd. The jukebox in the corner played the last few chords of "Sweet Home Alabama" before crackling as it shifted to the next track and "Simple Man" played. Someone was on a Lynyrd Skynyrd kick. Henry lowered his head and shuffled through the approaching crowd, aiming for the bar on the other side of the room.

Just as Skynyrd was singing "listen closely to what I say", the room erupted into chaos as everyone hurled questions toward Henry and Pete. Everyone but Daniel Williams, cousin to that piece of shit Robert Williams, and former overnight guest at the hunting lodge. He had been with the crowd that morning at the barn. Daniel now sat at the bar, his stool half-turned toward the front door, and a shit-eating grin on his face.

Easton Falls was a small town, and Henry liked almost everything about it. Except, as the current situation highlighted, the fact that gossip spread faster than the plague and it looked like Daniel had happily told everyone in the bar what had gone on over at the hunting lodge that morning. Or like any of the other dozen men who were there had talked. It didn't matter anymore who started it; Henry just hated the attention it was bringing down on him. Despite his obvious desire to just make it to the fucking bar for one goddamn pint, the questions and accusations flew at him rapid-fire.

"Is it true?"

"Is it Bigfoot?"

"Did you really shoot Bigfoot?"

"No fucking way it was Bigfoot."

"Does Kellen know?"

"Man, I gotta buy you a beer!"

Henry paid attention to that last one and zeroed in on the friendly voice. Before he could say "Gimme a Shiner," the crowd shifted, and he saw the faces of Conner Anderson and Lowell Hewitt. Lowell worked with Conner over at the Police Station, but it looked like both had already clocked out for the night since they were wearing civilian clothes and had half-drunk bottles of beer in front of them. It was Lowell who had offered the beer.

"Get the fuck out of my way," Henry snarled at the group around him. "Shit."

The disappointed crowd thinned, mumbling about what an asshole Henry was. Like he gave a shit what they thought.

He turned to Pete and gestured toward the other end of the bar where the two men sat. By the time Henry pulled up a stool, the bartender was popping the top off a bottle of Shinerbock, setting the beer down in front of him, and asking Pete if he wanted his usual.

Henry tipped his bottle at Lowell. "Thanks for the beer."

"No problem," answered Lowell. "But I gotta ask...did you really shoot a Bigfoot?"

Henry took a long swig of his beer before setting it back on the bar and wiping his mouth with the back of his hand. He took a deep breath and turned toward Lowell.

"I think so. Sure fucking looks like it, anyway." Henry glared at Conner. "Guess that shit got around pretty fast?"

Conner answered, "Yeah, and don't look at *me* like that. Daniel's been in here for the past hour telling everyone who would listen. You'd think *he* was the one to bring it in from the way he was bragging."

"Asshole," whispered Henry into his bottle. "It's not like I meant to. I thought it was a fucking bear."

"Well, it wasn't. Did you end up taking it to O'Malley's?" Conner asked.

"Yeah, I called him right after I hung up with you. Fucker's charging me an arm and a leg to keep it there, can you believe that?"

Pete leaned forward past Henry to see Conner on the other side of him. "I'm just happy there was a place for it besides my barn. Dottie's still bitching about the smell in there."

"Does it smell that bad?" Lowell asked.

"Yes," Pete and Henry answered in unison.

Conner chuckled. "Man, what I wouldn't give to have seen the look on O'Malley's face when he saw that thing. It's still there, right? Can we go see it?"

Henry shook his head. "No. I just want to sit here for one minute and not talk about that thing, or Kate, or anything else. The only thing I wanna talk about is who's buying the next round."

"Kate? What happened with Kate?" Lowell asked.

Conner called the bartender over to where they were sitting. "Hey Becca, this round's on me. Put it on my tab?"

She nodded and turned to the cooler behind her.

They were on their fourth round when Kellen Tsosie came into the bar, looked around, and beelined straight for them. He was panting as if he had been running and his eyes were wide and dead-set on Henry as he strode across the room. Henry sat sideways on the barstool and watched from the corner of his eye. He was never one to like having his back to the door. Any door. He knew it came from his Army days, times when you were on patrol and didn't know who your enemy was until they started firing at you. Or when you cleared buildings and had to evaluate everyone in every room you entered within seconds, or you were a dead man. It was a hard habit to break, even as a civilian, and Henry had just accepted that he would always be that way. But at that moment, Kellen wasn't a threat. He was determined, and serious about something, but not a threat.

Henry turned to face Kellen fully and raised his eyebrows. "Hey, Kellen. You ok?"

The older man paused a moment to catch his breath. "I've looked everywhere for you!"

"Well, here I am."

"You have to return it. Everything will be okay if you just return it." Kellen whispered cryptically.

"What the hell are you talking about? Return it? To the mountains? It's *dead*, Kellen." Henry answered, confused.

Conner, Lowell, and Pete spun their barstools around to

see what was going on as Kellen leaned closer to Henry. "Take it back, where it belongs. I can make it right, but it needs to go back before they'll even listen to me," He wiped the sweat from his eyes. "*If* they'll even listen to me."

Henry placed his hand on Kellen's shoulder. "Old man, how much have you had to drink?"

"I'm not drunk! You have to *listen* to me!" Kellen's voice crackled as he tried to keep from yelling.

Conner and Lowell stepped down from their stools and Conner said, "Kellen, I think it's time for you to leave."

Kellen backed up toward the door with his hands up between them. "I'll leave, but I *need* to talk to you, Henry. You know this is bigger than they think it is. You have to know that." His eyes darted between the off-duty officers and Pete.

"All I know is, you're awfully worked up over something you know nothing about." Henry was losing his patience as the beer and the day's stress were sinking in.

"I do know! You have to—" Kellen's cries were cut off as Conner and Lowell dragged him outside the bar.

"What was that all about?" Pete asked Henry.

"Fuck if I know," Henry swallowed the last of his beer and grabbed the next one from in front of him. "And fuck if I care about anything besides my tab right now. And I care shockingly little about *that*." He chugged most of the beer, set it on the table, and turned to Becca. "Another round, on me."

10

Henry leaned back in the chipped and faded rocking chair on the front porch of Jensen's General Store. The Game Warden, David Gregory, was waiting for him over at O'Malley's, but Henry wasn't in any hurry to get there. He wanted to enjoy a few more moments of peace before another weird-ass day descended upon him once again. He took a swig of his coke and wondered how everything had gone to hell in such a short amount of time.

The entire thing was a cluster-fuck, that much he was certain of. The night before, after they escorted Kellen from the bar, Conner and Lowell had paid the tab and taken off, groaning about having to work the next morning. Henry and Pete opened a new tab and ended up closing the place down. Henry told Pete everything. His reaction was almost as bad as Henry's had been. Henry and Kate were the perfect couple, starting the perfect life together. As perfect as a fucking heart attack. Pete was still shaking his head over the whole mess when Dottie showed up to take them home.

Henry fed Jager, his Great Dane, and they both fell asleep on the couch. The bed was still too cold and empty for Henry to lie on. He had thought of Pete and Dottie back at the cabin, getting ready for bed themselves, and going over how sad Henry's life had become. Fucking fantastic.

He opened his eyes around 10:00 a.m. the next day to Jager standing over him, her way of waking him up. It had been cute when she was a small-ish puppy, but at a hundred and forty pounds, it wasn't so cute anymore. He let her outside, started the coffee pot, and jumped into a much-needed shower. But Henry couldn't stand being in the house without Kate, so he took himself down to Jensen's for a hot dog and a coke before he had to tackle any more of his problems that day.

That's where he was sitting when a black van with dark windows sped by, splashing through the mud on the main road. Henry sighed and brought the bottle to his lips, savoring the last of the cold drink before wiping his chin and tossing it into the trash can with a thud. He'd never seen that van in town before, and it definitely wasn't David. He had been driving the same old piece-of-shit Chevy pickup for the last two years. Probably longer, but Henry couldn't attest to that since he himself had only been back in the States for a little over two years.

Henry straightened his cap and stood up. O'Malley's sat four blocks south, and he intended to walk as slow as possible to get there. A cool wind blew in from the coast, keeping the temperatures down into the 40's. The mess with the creature couldn't have come at a worse time. But maybe he should appreciate the distraction. Kate was staying with her parents over on Pine Street, in her childhood home. He glanced in that direction as he passed the intersection, and could feel his blood pressure rising. Unbelievable, that she would cheat on him. Outrageous, that she would let him think the baby was his.

What a *bitch*.

Henry was half a block past the Police Station when he finally heard, "Hey! I'm talking to you!"

He turned around to find Robert Williams standing behind him, cheeks red from the cold, or anger, he couldn't tell which. Henry stared at him, waiting. Given enough rope, men like Robert usually ended up hanging themselves.

"So?"

Henry took a deep breath. "So? So *what*? What are you talking about?"

"Listen, shit-for-brains, and I'll say it slower. Dottie's not here to save you this time. Are you ready to settle this, man to man?" Robert tensed, his body wound like a deer ready to pounce.

Behind Robert, and a few yards away, the front door of the Police Department opened, and Conner stepped out. Robert's back was to the officer, and he didn't hear the door. Only Henry knew Conner was nearby and could hear everything they were saying.

"Yeah?" Henry whispered too low for Conner to hear, "And what are *you* gonna do about it, asshole? *Punch* me? Come on, little bitch, let's see what you got."

Robert lunged, his fist swinging toward Henry's face. Henry could smell the alcohol on Robert's breath and the drink made him slower than usual. Even after a few beers himself, Henry would have no problem taking down a piece of shit like Robert Williams. Henry dodged the blow and returned a few of his own. A knee to the groin made Robert lean forward and grab his crotch, leaving his face wide open. Henry threw a series of rapid punches, all connecting with various parts of Robert's face until he dropped to his knees. Henry regained his composure and stepped back.

The Army had taught him a lot, but rage suppression was something he had to teach himself.

"You broke my nose!" Robert squealed around palms cupped in a poor attempt to catch the blood flowing onto the pavement.

"What the hell, Henry?" Conner yelled at his friend.

"Self-defense. You saw him swing at me first!" Henry proclaimed.

Conner sighed and yanked Robert's hands behind his back. "Get up, Robert." Handcuffs clinked as Conner locked them onto Robert's wrists. "I'm gonna do you a favor since you seem to have a death wish today."

"He told me to punch him! You heard him!" Robert screamed, wriggling to get free from the cuffs.

"I didn't hear shit, but I *did* see you swing at Henry and you're about three sheets to the wind. Let's go sit this one out in the tank." Conner jerked Robert toward the police department. "And Henry, get your ass to the butcher shop, everyone's waiting on us. Tell 'em I'll be right there."

Thankful that he didn't do any more damage to the asshole, Henry chuckled to himself. It was that easy. Robert was an idiot. As he walked toward the door of the butcher shop, he passed two black vans parked side by side. Both suspiciously nondescript, but for the long antennae protruding from their roofs and the pitch-black tint covering the windows. A far cry from David's Chevy parked next to them atop a growing pool of leaking engine oil.

David stood at the door to the butcher shop, wearing a two-day-old uniform and stinking of rotting flesh.

"What took you so long? I told you on the phone to be here by two."

David moved aside to let Henry through the doorway

before poking his head out, searching the parking lot. "Where's Conner?"

Henry covered his nose and walked into the butcher shop. "Handling some police business, he'll be right back. Shit, David, you reek."

"Yeah, you would too if you spent the last few days doing what I did. Now let's get this done so I can go home and take a shower. I haven't seen my dog in a week."

David followed Henry through the front door and smack into the middle of a heated discussion between O'Malley and a short, stocky woman Henry had never seen before. Her brown hair was pulled into a low ponytail, and she wore brand-new jeans that still had the crease down the front of both legs. She looked like the kind of woman who was used to wearing suits, standing too rigid and formal in her jeans, T-shirt, and tennis shoes. But she was holding her own as Richard O'Malley screamed at her.

"... am I supposed to do to feed my family, huh? I got paying customers talking about moving their business over to Plueville because they don't wanna buy meat that's been hangin' in the same room as this... this... manky *thing*! It's not even wrapped properly or cleaned! Just thrown in here like my freezer is the local dump!" The tips of his ears were crimson, and his balled fists struggled to stay at his sides. "When are you guys gonna get this shit outta here?!"

The woman replied in a steady, even tone, "Mr. O'Malley, I *am* sorry for the inconvenience, but you need to understand the importance of this. I assure you we'll be out of your way as soon as possible."

"This is bullshit. I pay taxes, you know! I pay your salary!" Richard turned to Henry, now standing beside them. "And you! This is *your* fault. You couldn't just leave well enough alone, could you! Now look at this!" He spread his arms out wide, encompassing the hairy unknown thing in the walk-in freezer and the three people inspecting it. The woman had apparently brought along a few friends.

Henry avoided Richard's stare. He *had* caused quite a mess. If he hadn't wandered so far off the trail, he wouldn't have come across the creature. It would still be alive, and Henry would have had a full night's rest. Instead, he was making do with just a few hours of fitful sleep, waking to some bullshit with Robert, and his arms and back felt like he'd been through the wringer. Nothing like hauling Bigfoot around the forest to get you into shape.

"O'Malley, why don't you head on home? I'll keep an eye on things here for you." David offered.

He glared once more at the woman in front of him before stalking out, cursing obscenities beneath his breath with every pound of his foot against the hard tile floor. He stopped at the entrance and turned to the group inside.

"You're a thick one if you think I'm leaving shit for you guys to *look after*, I'm staying right here outside until you all go back home." With that, he shoved the front door open and stomped to the edge of the curb. Sitting down, he turned halfway, keeping one eye on the street and one eye on the shop.

Henry looked at David with an eyebrow raised. David shrugged and proceeded with the business they had all come for. "Henry, this is Victoria Perez. Her people are in the cooler, inspecting the animal. Can you tell her exactly what happened?"

Henry shook Victoria's outstretched hand. "I'll tell you what fucking happened. I shot Bigfoot."

Victoria sighed pointedly, dropped her hand, and stared at him.

"Oh, I *know*... it's a 'creature' or some kind of 'deformed ape', but you know as well as I do that it ain't, or you wouldn't be up here snooping around. How exactly did you find out about this anyway, and who are you again?" Henry stared at Victoria.

"I'm with the Wildlife Department, and it doesn't matter how we know, but no. No one called us. Sometimes we... monitor... the game warden's calls to keep an eye out for anything unusual." She met his stare, unblinking.

"Wildlife Department, my ass," Henry mumbled. "Are you hearing this crap, David?"

David took a deep breath to calm himself. "Yeah, I hear it. It's bullshit, but I hear it."

"Why don't we go in the office and talk about this quietly," Victoria gestured to O'Malley's back room, a compact space tucked away behind the steel counter; the entrance marked by a low swinging door.

Henry followed them to the office as the bell rang over the front door and Conner entered the butcher shop. "Great timing, we're heading to O'Malley's office," Henry said. "And thanks for..." He jerked his head in the direction of the parking lot.

"Yeah, no problem. But really, you should stop antagonizing him."

"Now, where's the fun in that?"

"Took you long enough, Conner, I don't have all day," David muttered as he walked through the swinging door to the office.

David gestured for Victoria to sit in the chair behind the desk.

"No thanks, I'll stand," she said, leaning against a tall bookshelf. "So, Henry..." she looked down at her notes, "... Miller? Tell me exactly what happened out there."

David sat in O'Malley's chair, and Henry and Conner

occupied the two fold-up chairs in front of the desk, while Henry recounted the details from his trip.

"So, you didn't see anything else out there? Didn't hear anything?" Victoria flipped through her notes without looking up at Henry.

"Just the usual forest shit. I could have sworn when we were headed back to camp that I saw something behind us. But there was a storm, and the lightning was firing, playing tricks on the eyes, so it's hard to say. You don't... you don't think there's more of them out there?"

"There's no way to say, but the chances are likely."

"Shit," mumbled Henry before turning to David. "You said you saw the cattle over in League City yesterday, think this thing could have done that?"

David answered, "No, that was a pretty open-and-shut case. The Paxton sisters killed a mountain lion this morning and the claw marks matched up—"

Victoria interrupted, "So what we'll do is this, I'll send some of my guys out there, with you, of course, to show them where you were hunting, and we'll search the area for anything... out of place. Until then, I would suggest you try to calm down any talk of this *Bigfoot* stuff."

"Oh, you've got me fucked if you think I'm going back out there. Legend or not, I'm not interested in running into anything else... 'out of place'. That's fucking Sasquatch or Bigfoot or whatever the fuck you want to call it in there and you fucking know it."

Conner nodded in agreement, but David argued, "Now, you know there's no such thing as Bigfoot. That thing is clearly a mutation, a one-off." He turned to Victoria. "I'll go with you and your men into the woods to prove it."

Henry argued, "I'm still not—"

Kate's voice interrupted, squawking from the radio on Conner's chest. "*Dispatch to 502.*"

Henry paused, grimacing at the sound of her voice. It was the first time he'd heard it since their fight. Since she left him.

Conner reached across his chest and grabbed the radio clipped to his uniform shirt. "502 to dispatch, go ahead."

"*We've got a 10-54 over at Coopers' barn, Sean just called it in.*"

"10-4, 502 is 10-76."

Conner turned to the others. "You guys good here? I'm gonna go check this out." He left the office, the small door swinging behind him as he passed the front counter and headed toward the front of the shop.

"I'll come with you," David said as he hurried to catch up with Conner.

"What about my guys?" Victoria called after them.

David's voice grew smaller as he neared the front of the shop. "This shouldn't take long. I'll call you when we're done, and we can meet up over at the hunting lodge. O'Malley out front can give you directions."

Conner glanced back at David with a frown. "Well, you're ridin' in the back. You smell like shit."

David glared at him. "I'm taking my own truck."

Henry followed the other two, leaving before Victoria could ask him any more questions or try to get him to do anything else in those woods. He didn't care where they were going, as long as it was far away from her and her team. He jogged to his truck and grabbed his 9mm and holster before jumping into Conner's Jeep.

They were backing out of the parking lot when Conner slammed on his brakes. Standing in their path was Kellen Tsosie.

"What the fuck, Kellen? Do you have a death wish? I almost smoked you!" Conner yelled.

"Don't go. Just... don't go. Please, I'll fix it."

"What are you fucking talking about? We're kind of in a hurry here."

"Get the animal out of the shop and leave it here." Kellen gestured to the parking lot.

Conner stared at him. "Why? Why on earth would I want to do that?"

"Please. I beg you. That's all they want."

"Move the fuck away from my jeep before I run you over or arrest you for interfering with an investigation."

Kellen stepped aside, still pleading with the men to stop while the Jeep pulled out of the parking space. Conner glared at him as he slammed into first gear and sped out of the parking lot, splashing water onto the vehicle and almost spilling Henry out as he bounded through the potholes.

"Jesus, Conner... take it easy!" Henry yelled as he grabbed onto the frame of the Jeep.

Conner kept his eyes on the road. "That guy gives me the fucking *creeps*."

11

Sean Cooper lived with his parents in a small house at the edge of the woods, about halfway between the edge of town and the Stewarts' hunting lodge. Chickens scattered when Conner and David pulled up beside each other in front of the house. It was tidy and clean with light blue wooden siding and bright white trim. Concrete steps led to a wide front porch that wrapped around one side of the house. Once they cut their engines, a high-pitched whine emanated from beneath the porch. Peeking out from around a hole in the white lattice wood were two paws and a quivering wet snout.

Conner reached for his radio. "502 to dispatch, I'm 10-23 at the Coopers."

"*10-4, need backup?*" Kate asked.

"Negative, hold tight for now."

The men ignored the puppy and hurried around the back of the house to an old barn, its once-bright red paint sun-faded to pale pink. Conner stopped a few feet from the barn doors. Sitting in front of the barn was Sean Cooper.

"In there," Sean pointed. "I closed it back up, I didn't want..." he faltered, then dropped to his knees and sobbed.

"You stay back," Conner said to Sean while waving Henry and David over to him. They spread out, and Conner lifted the metal latch spanning the front entry of the barn. As they pulled open the heavy red doors, a sickly sweet odor assaulted them from within. The men exchanged looks. They knew that smell. It was the smell of death, like an animal caught in a trap for weeks, or the dumpster behind O'Malley's butcher shop.

Conner turned to Sean, "Stay right there, son."

Sean didn't argue. He'd already seen too much in that barn. Shivering from the cold and shock, he stared into the darkness beyond the barn doors.

Shafts of sunlight pierced the dusty air, landing on a single shoe sitting alone a few inches from the door. Dark red swatches lay scattered around the dirt floor of the building, leading off into the shadows. Conner inched closer to the lone shoe and recoiled, gagging. Nestled snugly inside, still contained by blood-spattered white laces tied neatly in a bow, sat a human foot. Or, the remains of one. Something had sheared it off above the ankle in a ragged tear.

Henry stepped inside while Conner followed and attempted to regain his composure. As their eyes adjusted to the dim interior of the barn, another shoe came into focus. But instead of a foot, it was attached to a leg; pulled apart from the body just below the knee. Nearby, a torso had been flung into the corner of the barn like a bale of hay, but drenched in blood. An apron clung loosely around it, bits of flour mingling with the blood to form a thick pink paste. It was Mary, Sean's mother. Gagging, Henry barely made it past the doors and into the sunlight before heaving the contents of his stomach onto the grass. Bits of partially digested hot dog stared up at him from a slush of cola and stomach acids, and he knew it would be a long while before he would be able to eat another one.

They found the father's torso later, in another corner.

Once the ambulance and other officers arrived, Conner turned the scene over to them while he and Henry focused on Sean.

"I know this is gonna be hard, but I need you to tell us exactly what happened. We need to find the animal that did this." Conner said as he sat next to Sean on a bale of hay and placed his hand on Sean's shoulder.

"Mr. Anderson... it wasn't no animal," Sean swiped the back of his hand across his tear-streaked cheeks and looked up at Conner. "It was *monsters*."

"Now Sean, you know there's no such thing—"

"I saw 'em. It was two giant monsters, hairy all over and smelly. I was hidin' behind the bales at the top. Dad wanted me to re-stack 'em 'cause they fell over."

"You were in the barn by yourself?"

"No. Well... yes. At first. Then Dad came in to clean out the horse stalls. We was both in there workin'."

"Then what happened?"

"Mom came in to tell us dinner was almost ready and then—" Sean's next words jumbled together as he sobbed.

Henry knelt and locked eyes with the boy. "Look here, Sean. I know what it's like to see some rough things. To see bad things happen to people you love. And it sucks. It does. It's not fair, and it sucks. And I know it's hard to think about it, but if you think you can... we need to know what happened so we can try to keep it from happening to someone else."

Sean nodded and cleared his throat. "I can do it."

"All right, buddy. So, your mom came into the barn..."

Conner led Sean back to the barn and the awful things that had happened there.

"She said dinner was almost ready, and she made apple pie. That's my favorite. It's prob'ly still in the kitchen... but I don't want it now." Sean paused, took a deep breath, and continued. "She was standin' there talkin' to dad when the doors flew open. She only opened one of 'em, you know. So the other one was... kinda closed. Does that part matter?" He looked up at Conner.

"Just whatever you can remember, it's all helpful."

"Okay. So, the other door banged open real loud, and a monster came in. It hit dad and made him fly all the way to the other side of the barn. Mom screamed, and I tried to get down to help her, but the monster had knocked the ladder down. I couldn't help her..." Sean's shoulders shook as he covered his face and cried again.

"It sounds like the animal was strong, it's good that you were up high, and it couldn't see you. If you had gone down to help your mom, you might have been attacked, too. You did the right thing in staying where you were."

Sean wiped the tears from his face and continued. "The first one came in and hit dad, like to get him out of the way or somethin'. It was sniffin' around like it was lookin' for somethin'. That's when the other one came in. It was more brown, but it was hairy and smelly just like the first one."

"More brown? What color was the first one?"

"Kinda red... like brown-red."

"Okay. Keep going, if you can."

"So, the second monster comes in, and that one was sniffin' and lookin' around too."

"And your mom was still there?"

"Yeah, she was screamin' and tryin' to help dad get up."

"Okay."

"So, the first one, like, remembers mom is there or just saw her or somethin', and picks her up like she's a toy. Like, grabs her and..." Sean looked up at Conner, his chin quivering, "...tore her apart like she was a paper doll. Then mom stopped screamin'..."

"You can do this, you're doing great."

"So, then it started throwin' pieces of her around the barn like it was mad about somethin'. But we didn't do anythin', I swear! Dad didn't even have a chance to shoot 'em. Why did they hurt them?"

Henry looked at Conner, confused. Animals didn't behave like that. Tearing people apart and flinging them around. But monsters didn't exist...

Conner answered, "I don't know, Sean. I don't know."

Henry rested his hand on the boy's small shoulder. "What happened to your dad?"

"He didn't wake up. From when the red one threw him across the barn. Do you think he was dead? That would have been good... to not feel what they did next."

"What did they do next?"

"The red one picked him up and shook him real hard. Then the brown one went over and they both just..." Sean dropped his face into his hands again. "They just grabbed him and pulled him apart. There was so much blood."

"Did the... *monsters*... see you?' Henry asked as Conner stood there shaking his head, dumbfounded.

"I screamed. I tried to be quiet, but I couldn't help it. One of 'em ran to me, the brown one, but stopped when it saw me sittin' up there," Sean pointed at the barn, up to the loft. "It looked right at me, then turned around and grunted at the other one, like they was talkin' but I couldn't tell. Then, they just left like nothin' happened. I stayed up there 'til I thought they were gone. Then I climbed down the other side and ran to the house."

"You are one lucky kid.' Conner blurted out before he could think about the words and the carnage Sean had just witnessed.

Henry glared at Conner, then sat down next to Sean on the hay bale and wrapped his arms around him.

"You were very brave. Your parents would have been very proud, and I am sure they would be glad you could tell their story. We *will* find these monsters buddy, you can count on that."

"Sean? Oh, *Sean*..." Theresa, Sean's Aunt, ran around the side of the house and scooped him up into her arms. Her face blotched red from crying. "I got you, it's all going to be okay. Let's get you out of here."

Shaken, Conner and David stood outside while Henry led a cleanup crew through the barn. That sort of thing was technically Conner's job, but Henry had a better stomach for it. Conner pulled a cigarette from his pack, his quivering fingers finally lighting it on the third try.

He handed the open pack to David. "Think this is still a rogue bear?"

David thought about it and lit a cigarette. He stared at the crew around the barn before answering. "Bears don't do this," he whispered after taking a long drag and exhaling a cloud of smoke.

"No, bears don't do this." Conner agreed, his eyes still locked on the carnage in the barn. "What if... okay, just hear me out here. What if that thing sitting in O'Malley's freezer isn't the only one? What if there's more? What if that bitch Victoria and the kid are right about that?"

"Sean is clearly traumatized. Shit, if a bear tore my

parents apart when I was his age, I would say they were big hairy monsters, too."

"But what if those rumors about Kellen and the other Tsosies *are* true, and we've got a pissed-off tribe of Bigfoot out for revenge? Bigfoots? Bigfeet? Whatever the fuck you call 'em." Conner asked.

"What rumors? You know I don't pay attention to any of that shit."

"Jesus, David. How can you live here and not know about this?"

"Like I said... I still think the kid is going through some stuff and it's a bear. Or two."

Conner grabbed David's shoulders, forcing the other man to look at him. "Look, I know it sounds crazy, but just hear me out, ok?"

"Fine."

"The Tsosie's have been here longer than anyone else. Their entire family has. I'm talking native Kwakiutl here," Conner began.

"I knew that," huffed David.

"Okay, so there've been rumors forever that they've got this big secret, something to do with the Kwakiutl Indians. At one time they split up into two tribes, and one of them moved further north, but the other tribe stayed here and lived close to the Cascades. That's just history, that's not a secret."

"*Everyone* knows the Kwakiutl live by the Cascades. Kwakiutl aren't monsters." David rolled his eyes, in no mood for a history lesson.

"Shut the fuck up and listen," Conner's voice sharpened. "So, apparently, there was another tribe living at the foothills, something more ancient than even the Kwakiutl. They called 'em the Dzunukwa."

"Now you're just making up words. Besides, isn't that the big hairy thing that carries kids around in a basket to eat them?"

Conner sighed. "Jesus, David. Think outside the box, here. Those stories are like... half-truths. So, the Kwakiutl and the Dzunukwa were able to live together in peace, because of something the Tsosies had a hand in. And that's where it gets fuzzy, but legend has it that Kellen's family is the key to keeping this peace together."

"That sounds ridiculous. Are we done with fairy-tales now?" David asked.

"Look, all I'm saying is think of what Sean described, think of what happened to his parents. Shit, you saw the bodies! You know bears don't do that."

"I agree there. I don't think a bear did that. But as for anything else..." David stared at the barn. "I just don't know."

———

When the last pieces of Sean's parents were bagged and tagged, and Sean had gone home with his aunt, Conner and Henry slowly climbed back into Conner's Jeep. David stood next to his truck, facing the other two men. They waited for the coroner's van to clear the driveway.

"What. The. Fuck." David muttered.

Henry didn't answer. He'd seen plenty of awful things and waste of human life in the war. The things men could do to each other had hardened him, but that barn... that was no man. You could reason with a man and predict what he would do next. But a creature that no one knew anything about, *that* scared the shit out of him.

David stared into the woods, still hoping for some sign

of a bear because anything else would leave more questions than answers. "I don't even know what animal would have the strength needed to rip a body apart like that. Maybe a gorilla... "

Conner turned the key in the ignition. "Hey, do you mind if we swing by Wren's? These bears, or whatever we're dealing with, they're dangerous and we need to warn him to stay inside. I tried calling, but the old fucker won't answer his phone. He's the closest house out here."

David mumbled, "Definitely a bear. Or..."

"Dammit guys, you know what this is. It's not some 'rogue bear'. It's fucking *Bigfoot*. Call it what it is," Henry stared at the other two men. "But the real question is... why here? Why this barn?"

They sat in contemplative silence before Henry had an idea. "Anthony Cooper was at the lodge this morning. He was one of the guys touching the animal I shot in Pete's barn. What if... what if they *smell* him or something?"

"I'm not sure what it is, if it even *is* anything besides some lone freak of nature. What you have over at the butcher shop... that's one thing. Probably some bear who drank the water back when Kinney's Plant was pouring all their run-off into the stream. A one-off. What happened back at the barn... I have no idea. This is out of my area of expertise." David tapped the hood of the jeep, "But you guys head out, I'm gonna meet Ms. Perez and the team over at the hunting lodge, see what we can turn up."

"Be careful out there," Henry warned.

"You too."

12

Conner turned right onto a dusty, beaten path. Two parallel grooves in the dirt marked the way through an increasingly thick patch of trees. The men bumped along in silence, both lost in their thoughts. In the span of a few days, Henry's world had been turned upside-down, and he still hadn't had time to process it all. Conner, usually the one to make a joke of everything, remained silent.

"You all right?" Henry asked.

"What? Yeah..." Conner glanced at Henry before facing the road again. "Just a lot of shit going on, you know?"

"Tell me about it. Oh man, I haven't even had a chance to tell you what happened with Kate."

Conner gripped the wheel tighter as they passed over small limbs and potholes.

"I proposed."

"Yeah?" Conner asked, keeping his eyes on the road.

"She said no. And that's not even the worse part." Henry watched the trees fly by as they drove. "The baby isn't mine."

"Really? Man, that sucks."

Henry's eyes narrowed as he stared at Conner. "That's all you got, 'That sucks'?"

"What do you want me to say, man? It sucks." Conner glanced at Henry before turning back to the road.

"Fuck, Conner... did you know? Why didn't you say something, man? I would have told you some shit like that!"

Conner hesitated before answering. "Yeah, I knew... I didn't know how to tell you."

"Shit," Henry answered. "Well, I'm gonna fucking kill him, whoever it is," Henry paused, then turned to Conner. "Wait, how did you know? Who told you?"

"Hey, we're here."

A modest blue house emerged around the next turn. Smoke curled from the chimney, whispering into the ominous clouds above. The screen door at the front of the house banged in the breeze, flashing views of a darkened hallway beyond. They pulled up next to old man Wren's rusty pickup truck and cautiously scanned the area around the house before climbing out of the jeep.

"Hey, you hear that?" Henry whispered. They both froze, listening.

"Hear what? The door banging?" Conner asked.

"No. Not the door, everything else."

Conner cocked his head to the side. "I don't hear anything."

"That's just it. There's nothing. No birds, no crickets, no frogs... *nothing*."

Conner flipped the safety off his pistol and slowly turned toward the tree line at the edge of Wren's property. The sun hung low in the sky, peeking out between clouds and casting golden beams between the firs. Shadows danced and morphed as the men held their breath and stared into the woods.

Nothing. No sounds, no animals moving about. Only silence.

Conner shook his head and tucked his handgun back into the holster at his hip. "Jesus, this shit is creeping me out. Let's just check on Wren and get the hell out of here."

"Deal."

They jogged to the front porch and banged on the door frame. "Wren! You in there? It's Henry Miller and Conner Anderson!" Henry yelled into the empty hallway. Nothing came from the house in response but a vague sense of unease, wafting around them like a bad dream.

"I'm going in. Henry, stay out here and look out for... fuck, just look out."

"Screw that, I'm going with you," argued Henry.

Relief showed on Conner's face, though he would never admit it. He held the screen door open and they entered the house. A putrid, earthy scent permeated the entrance hall, cutting off the fresh fall air just a few feet away.

Conner flipped on the light switch by the kitchen, illuminating a strange scene in front of them. A teapot sat on the stove, long past the boiling point and smoking, the base of it burnt and blackened. Henry turned the heat dial to the off position and moved the pot, burning his fingers on the metal handle in the process.

He stepped back and fell, tripped by something laying on the linoleum behind him. Henry tried to catch himself but came face to face with Old Man Wren's watch. He knew it was Wren's because it was still attached to a liver-spotted arm, detached from Wren's body and laying there on the kitchen floor surrounded by broken glass.

"Conner..." Henry clambered to his feet and backed away from the arm. Conner came around the corner of the island and looked down. He whistled low, leaning against the table in the corner.

"Holy... "

"Jesus Christ," Henry interrupted, staring out the window over the sink and into the backyard. Rather, staring through the gaping hole where the window used to be, jagged pieces of glass were still stuck in the frame around the edges. Wren had a superb view from his back porch. A trim yard that he meticulously mowed every Saturday morning butted up to the tall spruce, hemlock, and fir trees at the edge of the Black Forest. The forest ran for miles until it touched on the edge of the Cascade foothills to the east. He had recently planted something in his vegetable garden, the dirt still darkened from the rainstorm the night before. Laying there, between the rows of seedlings sprouting proudly from the dirt and visible from the kitchen window, lay the remains of Old Man Wren. His head sat upright on the soil, eyes closed as if he had dug himself a little hole and taken a nap. On closer inspection, you could see the ground damp with blood around the edges of his neck that had been ripped ragged from his body. His torso lay twenty feet away, at the edge of the woods, as if it were flung there like a child's forgotten plaything, bleeding and still. The men turned in circles, inspecting the rest of the yard.

"Where's the rest of him?" asked Henry. "It has to be here... somewhere."

"I think I see something over by the road," answered Conner as he walked around the side of the house. He picked up his pace, glancing into the dense trees as he passed them. There, in the ditch by the entrance to the driveway, lay a single leg, shoe-less and bloody. "I don't know how we missed it coming in."

"We weren't exactly looking for loose limbs."

They scanned the area around the ditch

Henry finally whispered. "He was at the lodge, Old Man Wren. Right before we headed back to town yesterday. He was dropping off a load of fish. That's how he pays for his trips. We showed him the Bigfoot. He *touched* it...just like Anthony Cooper. I'm telling you, I bet they *smell* us." Henry shivered. "Let's get the fuck out of here. Those bastards could still be around."

Conner pulled the radio from his shirt and pressed the call button. The angry beep echoed around them in the silence. "502 to Dispatch, we're gonna need that van again, over at old man Wren's place. Send... everyone."

Silence.

The radio beeped as Conner tried again. "Dispatch? Kate? You there?"

Silence.

"Kate? Kate, are you there? Talk to me!" Panic rose in Conner's voice.

"Shit," Conner said before handing the radio to Henry. "The radios usually don't go out until just past the hunting lodge. But that's miles to the west. I got a bad feelin' about this. You keep trying, I'll drive."

The clouds rumbled and a light rain erupted from their depths, falling onto their shoulders as they ran back to the jeep, casting glances into the surrounding woods. The men held on to anything they could as Conner gunned it down the bumpy path toward the main road. The forest remained silent around them as Henry kept trying to reach Kate on the radio.

13

By the time they made the forty-five-minute drive back to town, the rapidly approaching night had devoured most of the sun and the light rain turned to a downpour.

"There's her car," Henry shouted over the clatter of the rain, holding onto the passenger door of the jeep as Conner whipped into the Police Station parking lot.

Parked in its usual place outside the small gray building that jointly housed the town's police department and municipal court, sat Kate's maroon Chevy.

Conner's jeep screeched into the parking spot next to her car and Henry jumped out before they rolled to a stop. He threw open the doors to the old building and ran through the lobby toward the hallway at the other end, closely followed by Conner. The station seemed empty. If it weren't for a half-empty cup of coffee and a still-warm pot on the counter, it would have looked like no one had been there all day. Chairs were pushed away from desks as if they had rolled there in a hurry, and papers lay scattered around the floor.

"Kate!" Conner yelled as he ran down the hallway after Henry.

Henry spun around the corner and threw the glass door to the Dispatch room open. The radios, usually squawking with activity and beeps, sat in silence. Kate Johnson, usually clacking away at the keyboard, head cocked sideways to hold a phone to her shoulder, was missing. The big armchair that usually sat behind the monitors had been turned onto its side.

"Shit."

"Henry, this doesn't mean anything. You know what *isn't* here?" Conner placed his hand on his best friend's shoulder.

"Any sign of Kate?" Henry answered.

"Exactly. Look around. No blood, no body. Not like the scene in the barn or Old Man Wren's. So, we're gonna assume she's somewhere safe and in one piece. She's smart —" Conner's voice broke.

"Yeah..." Henry hurried down the hallway.

They searched every office, bathroom, and storage closet, but couldn't find any sign of life.

"Hey! Are you gonna leave me in here all day? I didn't do nothing wrong, that fucker right there started it, and he knows it!" Robert Williams yelled from a dark corner of one of the drunk tanks, a small five-by-five cell occupied by a single bench and a toilet. He was propped up on one arm, lying prone on the bench and rubbing his eyes.

"You could at least give me some of that coffee..."

"Shit, I forgot all about him," Conner muttered, walking over to the steel bars. "Robert, what happened here?"

"I'll tell you, but first you let me out."

Henry flew across the room and reached through the bars before Robert could blink. He grabbed Robert's shirt collar and slammed his face into the steel bars with a sickening crunch.

"Quit your fucking games and tell us what happened. Now."

"What the fuck, man?" Robert pulled away as Henry's grip loosened. He wiped the blood from his nose and turned to Conner. "I know you saw that. That's assault!"

Conner leaned in close to Robert's face and asked pointedly, "What. Happened?"

Robert sighed. "Fine, I don't know what fucking happened. I was asleep on this hard-ass bench. Not even a blanket or a pillow—"

"Robert."

"I woke up to everyone running outside. That's all I know."

"Did you see Kate?" Conner asked, hope sparking in his eyes.

Henry's eyes bored into Robert's, fury spreading like a fever across his face, and waited to hear the answer.

"Yeah, right before everyone left, she said she was gonna go check on her mom and dad. But I don't know where everyone is. I swear it. They just left me in here to rot. I got rights, you know!"

"What the *Hell* is going on?" Conner sank into his chair, rolling it back a few inches and bumping into Officer Adam Martinez's desk behind him.

"I don't know... I don't understand any of this," muttered Henry.

"Kate." Conner's voice caught in his throat. "And the baby... oh, God." Conner leaned forward and put his hands on either side of his face. He looked up at Henry with tears hovering on his bottom eyelids, threatening to overflow.

Henry stared at him. "Until we find a body, I'm gonna

assume she's okay. Like you said, she's a smart girl. She'll know what to do."

"But, the baby..." Conner trailed off, wiping a tear from his face. He cleared his throat and looked around the empty station. Henry stared at his friend and his eyes narrowed.

"Hey! Let me the *fuck* out of here!" Robert screamed from his corner.

Henry and Conner ignored Robert's cries from across the room. Henry cocked his head to the side as he stared at Conner, waiting for him to face his direction. When their eyes met, Conner jumped.

"What?" Conner asked, turning away from Henry once again.

"Conner." Henry's voice hardened. "Look at me, Conner."

Conner slowly turned to face his friend but remained silent.

Years passed between them. Decades of friendship, history, family, and shared secrets. Hours spent on the diamond, pitching to one other. Summers camping in the Elba Forest with the Scouts, learning how to make a fire from nothing but twigs and moss. Weekends sleeping over at each other's houses, playing video games and eating pizza until they burst. They knew each other better than anyone. And, after playing poker together every Monday night over at Adam's place, Henry knew when Conner had a bad hand. And right then, Conner held the worst hand Henry had ever seen.

"Kate," Henry stated, not breaking eye contact.

Conner's face broke into a grimace and he didn't wipe away the tears that fell. "I'm *so* sorry, Henry. We didn't mean to, I *swear* to you—"

Henry jerked up from his perch on the edge of the desk

and stepped toward Conner, his fists clenching at his sides. A shrill ring of Conner's cell phone pierced the silence.

Shaking, Conner fumbled with the phone on his hip, glanced at the caller ID, and pressed the speaker button.

"Conner? Are you there?" David's voice echoed around the small room.

"David? I'm here. What did you find?" Conner and Henry stared at one another. Henry shaking with anger, and Conner, face pale and eyes wide.

"It's bad. You need to come out here." David's voice broke, and he took a deep breath.

"Are you still at the lodge? Is Ms. Perez with you?"

"No, they never showed up. I don't think. Their vans aren't here, and she isn't answering her phone."

"So, what's going on, then?"

"It's bad. This is way out of my jurisdiction, can you just get the hell out here?"

"What? What happened?!" Robert yelled from his spot in the dark corner of the cell as he jumped up from the bench and hurried to the bars.

"Would you shut up? David, are you in danger right now?" Conner asked.

"No, I don't think so. It's... I think I'm alone here. Well..." David broke down, sobbing into the phone.

"Okay. David, listen to me. Can you sit tight while I look for Kate and the other officers real quick? I'm not sure they're safe... "

At the sound of Kate's name, Henry unclenched his hands and collapsed into a chair, slouched and beaten. It didn't matter how angry he was, or hurt. By Kate or Conner. Nothing fucking mattered anymore.

"Well, it doesn't look like there's any trouble here, anymore. But whatever dropped in on the Coopers... well, it looks like it came here first. But fuck that, I'm not hanging around for one more second—"

Conner interrupted him. "David, you still got your Ruger?"

"Yeah, loaded and ready."

"Okay, keep your phone on you, and meet us at the butcher shop. We gotta check on a couple things first, but I have a feeling the answers we're looking for have to do with that thing Henry killed."

"Got it, see you soon," David said before disconnecting the line.

Conner grabbed a ring of keys from a hook on the wall and headed toward Robert's cell.

Henry stood up and walked to the large window at the front of the station, waiting until his back was to the other men before wiping a tear from his eye. Outside the double-paned glass, it seemed like a typical small town at dusk... except it wasn't. The buildings were the same, the cars parked along the street and in the lots were the same, but it was void of any *life*. No horns honking or doors slamming shut. The benches in front of the ice cream parlor across the street sat empty, no sticky-fingered children laughing while they licked their cones.

"Hold on," Henry walked to the door and peered outside.

Conner stopped a few feet from Robert's cell and turned around to face Henry.

"What do you see?" asked Henry, pointing to the street outside.

Conner walked to where Henry stood. He stepped through the doorway and out onto the sidewalk in front of the building where the small awning kept him dry from the

The Easton Falls Massacre: BIGFOOT'S REVENGE

storm. He scanned both sides of the street before answering. "Nothing. There's nothing but rain."

"Exactly. Where are all the *people*? The cars?"

The two men stood in silence, eyes narrowed as they tried to peer through the downpour at the empty town outside. One of the streetlights, shattered from a kid's baseball the week before, broke up the line of yellow lights along Main Street. A wind blew in from the north, bringing with it a familiar, musky odor. The small tree in front of them on the edge of the sidewalk swayed before righting itself again. Two buildings down, a curtain fluttered as a small hand pulled it closed from inside the ice cream shop.

Without a word, they stepped back into the building and closed the door.

Henry broke the silence with an exhaled, anxious breath. "I'm going to the Johnsons', that's where Robert said she was going. And I need to check on my mom. You coming?"

Conner hurried to the gun closet and took out two rifles, checked that they were loaded, and handed one to Henry.

"I also have my pistol," Henry said as he checked the rifle's safety. "Let's get these motherfuckers."

"What about me?" Robert yelled.

"You're fine," Conner called over his shoulder as he followed Henry out of the police department.

14

Henry and Conner walked in silence, scanning the side roads and ditches along the way to the Johnsons' house. Rain fell around them, thick and tense. At the intersection of Fir and Main, Henry stopped to face Conner.

"So."

Conner, a few steps ahead, turned and looked at his friend. His best friend.

"Henry, it's pouring down!"

"So."

Conner wiped the rain from his forehead and sighed, "I'm sorry, we both are. I swear we didn't mean for this to happen. It just... did."

"You don't get to speak for her. For Kate. You were with me when I picked out the fucking engagement ring!" Henry resumed walking, at a much faster pace than before. He shoved his hands in his pockets to keep himself from knocking Conner clean the fuck out.

Conner jogged to keep up, splashing through puddles forming on the street.

"Is it still *happening*?" Henry asked through gritted teeth, eyes on the road ahead of him.

Conner kept his head down. Whether it was against the rain or to keep from looking at Henry, only he knew.

"Goddammit, Conner. The whole time?"

"No. After that weekend in Seattle, we swore it would never happen again. We were drunk, Henry. We didn't want to hurt you, you *have* to believe that. But then, the baby..."

"I know he isn't mine." Henry interrupted.

"Yeah, she told me."

"Oh, isn't that fucking fantastic? 'She told me'. Guess you two are just the best of fucking friends now," Henry growled.

"What do you want me to say, Henry?" Conner pleaded.

"She's leaving you too, you know. Kate. She'll definitely move to Seattle now."

Conner didn't speak as they passed Spruce Street. They walked through the downpour, away from the lights of Main Street and into the darkness.

When they turned onto Monroe, Conner looked at Henry and yelled over the noise of the rising storm, "I'm going with her."

"When, exactly, were you going to tell me? When were you planning on telling me, either of you? When Otis... when the baby was born? Would you have really stood there and let me think I was his dad?"

"She should have told you long before that. I *wanted* her to tell you."

Henry took a step toward Conner and swung, his fist making impact with Conner's chin. Henry then turned around and kept jogging toward the Johnsons' house. Conner was on the pavement, hands on his jaw, staying down like a beaten dog. *Fucking perfect. Conner just took it. He saw the punch coming and took it because he knew he was a piece of shit and deserved it.*

The Johnsons lived in a red brick home on Monroe Street, three blocks from the Police Department. Betty Johnson's small red coupe and Clifford Johnson's black Chevy truck sat in the driveway. Perched on a branch high in the oak tree in the middle of the front yard was Monday, their orange tomcat. Cliff and Betty had planted the oak tree when they bought the house, ten years before they had Kate. Named for the day of the week they adopted her from the pound over in Lisyville, Monday hissed as they walked beneath the tree and swatted the air in front of him.

"I never liked that fucking cat," Henry muttered as they approached the front door.

Conner rubbed his jaw and scanned the street behind them while Henry knocked.

Silence.

He knocked again, rapping twice on the thick wooden door before trying the handle. It was open. Easton Falls was the kind of town you didn't have to worry about locking your doors, day or night. Though most people locked them at night anyway, ever since that bear over on Henderson managed to open the door and surprise Peter Washington while he rummaged through his refrigerator for a midnight snack. Wearing only his boxers, he had run screaming up the stairs to his bedroom, scaring the daylights out of his wife, Helen. They locked their bedroom door and used her phone to call the police station. They needn't have worried; they were the last things on that bear's mind. Since Peter had left the refrigerator door open, the bear was too busy helping himself to Mrs. Washington's leftover pot roast to worry about the people upstairs. Kate worked the lines that night, and she and Henry had laughed about it for weeks afterward.

Henry longed for the days when bears were the only beasts they had to worry about. He was still convinced it was two more Bigfoot creatures; friends, or family, or whatever, of the one he had killed. He couldn't shake the feeling he had set something in motion that no one was prepared to handle, and that wouldn't stop anytime soon. There was still more blood to spill.

The lights were on in the living room and kitchen. The TV flickered, grey lines danced across the screen and a steady static fuzz came from the speakers. The DVD player sat next to it, the small green light showing the power was on. They had been watching a movie. The remote lay on the floor next to Cliff's overstuffed recliner as if it had merely fallen off the arm when he got up to take a piss. Nothing about the room said there was trouble, and everything about the room said there was trouble. The kitchen was no different; the smell of beef, onions, and potatoes wafted from a crock-pot on the counter, the juices bubbling to the surface. A tasting spoon lay next to it on a small dish, brown gravy dripping from the spoon onto the white surface. On the table in the middle of the kitchen sat that afternoon's mail, but someone had opened only the top envelope. The sharp letter opener wasn't in its usual spot, and glass was on the floor, a cup shattered amongst a puddle of water. From the back of the house came a bubbling, wet noise.

Henry and Conner looked at each other, then stepped toward the kitchen, not speaking.

Kate's dad must have been watering the vegetable garden when it happened, the thing that they seemed to always be a step behind. The creatures destroyed everything in their path. Solar lights in the backyard illuminated a grisly scene. The hose spewed water, joining the rain and surrounding her dad's broken body with a muddy paste. Mr. Johnson was a small man when he was alive, and he seemed even smaller in death. That's what happened when you cut something into five pieces. His torso, laying so close to his legs it looked like they were still attached, wasn't actually attached to any part of his body. A hand, still wrapped around the water hose, lay by his side, the arm gaping at the shoulder where it had been yanked away. A foot sat a few feet away, the crew sock bunched around the toes and soaked with blood. His head, unlike Sean Cooper's parents, was still attached. Bright blue eyes stared up at the inky sky, forever locked on the falling rain, lifeless.

Henry leaned across the flowerbed and rotated the knob on the spigot to the water hose, the old steel squeaking as it turned off. His foot squished into the soft, wet ground.

"Jesus Christ," he whispered before glancing around the yard and backing up toward the house.

Whatever had done that, whatever was capable of that level of brutality, he knew he didn't want to run into it in the Johnsons' backyard. Conner stepped down from the back doorstep.

"Maybe they went to your mom's... shit!" His eyes fell on the mutilated corpse of Kate's dad.

"Get back in the house," Henry urged Conner through clenched teeth. "Now."

The two men eased back into the house and bolted the door behind them. Whatever was strong enough to do the things they'd seen, could get into that house; bolt or no bolt. But it was all they knew to do. Conner stood in the kitchen, a purple bruise forming on his jawline, the skin taut and shiny. He stared at the backyard through the window over the sink while Henry ran to Kate's old room, desperate to find her alive. They may not have had a future together, and he was hurt and angry over what she had done, but he couldn't flip the switch in one day. He had a ring. He thought they would be *forever* and he couldn't just turn off a history. *Their* history. He needed to make sure she was okay, then he would walk away from it all, never thinking of her again.

The door to her room was closed, a good sign. Henry jerked it open, scanning the room for any sign of danger or Kate herself.

It was empty.

The same bed she had slept on the night before, sat in front of him. The sheets were tucked in and the comforter laid across it neatly. A nightstand and a dresser, the only other pieces of furniture in the room, sat with gleaming surfaces, polished and with the scent of oranges still clinging to them. Kate's mom kept the room tidy, as she did the rest of her home. When Kate wasn't sleeping there, which hadn't happened since she had moved in with Henry, they used it as a guest room. They had always joked about it because her parents didn't know anyone who lived far enough away to need a place to stay. But Betty Johnson liked the idea of a guest room, so that's what it stayed. Cliff never cared enough to argue about it.

"Where's Kate?" asked Conner, standing in the doorway behind Henry.

Henry turned and went back into the living room, answering over his shoulder, "Not here. Any sign of Betty? She was probably in the house when Cliff was—" He couldn't finish the thought. "I don't know where either of them could be now. Unless they ran to my mom's..."

The two men stared at each other before they bolted through the front door, not bothering to close it behind them. They were long past the point of worrying about hungry, refrigerator-scavenging bears.

Henry's mom, Suzanne Miller, lived four houses down from the Johnsons in her own red brick house, though she had painted it white four years before. The men ran across lawns of the homes in-between, glancing at windows and doors, hoping someone would be home, but the street was dead.

"Noooooooooooooooooo!" Henry wailed as they ran closer and the front porch came into view, lit by a dim yellow haze from the lamp hanging above the door.

Conner grabbed Henry and spun him around. "You don't need to see this."

Henry fought him. "Get the fuck off me!"

"Henry!" Conner managed to get Henry to look at him. "You *don't* need to see this!"

Henry knew he was right. The glimpse he *had* seen had already burned onto the back of his eyelids so that even closing his eyes couldn't keep the vision of his mom's front porch out of his mind. Henry dropped to his knees on the front lawn and wailed.

In front of him, on the porch, sat the rocking chair that had been his grandmother's. The chair his mom had used to rock Henry to sleep when he was a baby, and his grand-mother had used to rock his mom to sleep before him. Four generations of Miller's had sat or slept in that chair. But Henry knew after that day, no one would ever again.

Sitting in the chair was his mom, or what used to be his mom. Even without a head, he knew it was her. Suzanne Miller sat in the rocker, her jeans stained with dirt from the garden and the T-shirt Henry had picked up for her at the Nationals game covered in blood. The previously white shirt was unrecognizable and above that, where her gold necklace should have hung, the one she had worn every day since Henry bought it for her before he left for Iraq, was nothing but a jagged, gaping hole.

Conner ran to the front porch, almost tripping on a large rock at the edge of the walkway. Except it wasn't a rock, it was Suzanne Miller's head, with her silver-grey hair, curly and cut short against her scalp. Conner leaned into the bushes bordering the porch and threw up everything he had eaten that day. It wasn't much; he had been too busy to stop and eat for most of it, so he dry-heaved until he could move away from the stench of blood, urine, and death.

Conner turned back to the front yard and yelled at Henry's back, "Stay there and don't turn around. I'll be right back."

Henry turned around. "No."

He jumped to his feet and ran up the front porch steps, turning his head away from the grisly scene, and pushed Conner out of the way.

Henry stepped onto the porch, freezing when the top board creaked beneath his weight. Every instinct in his body told him to run away from there as fast as he could. Hell, to run out of *town* as fast as he could. But he was in it, and he wasn't one to run away from a fight. He lifted his rifle and walked through the gaping hole in the side of the house where the front door once stood.

It was brighter than it should have been, considering the horrific scene on the front porch. Lights were on in the living room and kitchen, and the TV blared a rerun of *The Twilight Zone*. A portrait of Henry's dad hung crooked on the wall, and Henry touched it as he walked by, thinking it was better for his dad to have gone the way he did, instead of the violence that had claimed everyone else that day. A heart attack in his sleep, while not exactly peaceful, was still better than this.

Conner followed Henry into the house. The hallway looked as if a bull had torn through it; there were gouges in the walls from floor to ceiling, and the ceiling itself bowed upward, broken in several places. Musk hung in the air around them, hot and thick. They'd been chasing that goddamn smell all day. Bile rose in the back of Henry's throat as he crept along the hallway, listening for any sign of the creatures.

At the end of the hallway, in the doorway to Henry's old room, lay Kate's mother. Henry leaned against the shattered door frame, careful not to step on her bloody, outstretched hand. With a hand on Henry's back, Conner led him further into the room. They didn't have time to mourn.

If a bomb had dropped in the middle of Henry's childhood room, it would have caused less damage than what they were staring at right then. Barely recognizable, the mattress lay shredded and strewn about the room. Every piece of furniture had been crushed and a hole the size of a Chevy sat where his window overlooking the backyard used to be. Outside, shards of glass and wood lay on the ground and the wooden fence surrounding the yard had been ripped apart.

Kate was still missing.

15

A frigid wind blew in from the west, throwing leaves into the air around Henry and Conner as they ran to the butcher shop in silence. Henry was still rocked mute by the discovery of his mom. He knew it was his fault, everything that had happened. His fault for straying from the trail, for shooting the creature, for bringing the wrath of whatever those things were upon the town.

They seemed capable of strength unknown to any man. The things they had done... and for what? Revenge? An accident? Henry wasn't a violent man, not anymore. He wouldn't have killed the thing had he known it was... different. But it looked like a fucking bear.

The streets were silent but for a steady patter of rain and a few branches swishing in the breeze When the wind picked up, the metal traffic lights creaked and groaned from their wiring as they hung above the two men.

"Where is everyone?" Conner whispered.

"Fuck if I know... wait," A fluttering in a window across the street had caught his attention, a sliver of light showing

HOLLY RAE GARCIA & RYAN PRENTICE GARCIA

from inside the home. "Maybe they're all inside, and for the better. Let's just keep going."

When they arrived at O'Malley's Butcher Shop, it looked *almost* exactly as it had when they had left earlier that day. The two unmarked vans still sat conspicuously in front of the store, but the front door to the shop now sat atop one of the vans, bent and cracked with the attached bell tinkling in the wind. A hole at least four feet across gaped where the door had been. Kellen Tsosie sat on the bench outside, his head in his hands.

"Hey Kellen, you ok?" Conner touched the man's shoulder as Henry scanned the area around them, rifle at the ready, then peered through the hole in the front of the shop.

Kellen brought his head up and looked at Henry, ignoring Conner. "*You* did this, and there's nothing you or I can do to stop it. It has to play out now. It's too late."

Henry turned his attention back to Kellen. "What is *it*? What *are* they?"

Kellen dropped his head back into his hands and whispered, "You can't stop them. The only thing you can do is run and hope that they never find you," He looked up at Henry. "You killed their child."

"I didn't fucking know!" Henry cried.

"Yes, of course. No one ever knows how the things they do ripple through time. You've caused a lot of damage. I'm partly to blame, I knew he had strayed too far east. This is our fault, and right now we're dealing with two very large, and very pissed off, parents."

"How do you know all of this?" Conner asked.

"It doesn't matter. You two need to leave They have your scent, Henry. You'll never be safe here."

A woman's scream echoed from deep within the shop behind Kellen.

"Kate!" Henry shouted to Conner, "I'll take lead and you watch my back. Shoot anything that isn't human."

Tears flowed down Kellen's face, but he didn't move to wipe them away and remained sitting on the bench.

Conner nodded to Henry and pulled the stock of the rifle tight against his shoulder. Henry adjusted the sling of his rifle, allowing it to swing free if he needed it, and drew his pistol from the holster, pulling the slide back enough to see a shiny gold round in the chamber.

"Follow my lead," Henry whispered before crouching down and easing forward.

He felt a rush he hadn't experienced in years. Clearing a building, not knowing what was around the corner, was how he had paid the bills in his younger years. His breathing slowed, calm and deliberate. All at once he could feel the slightest bit of wind, hear the smallest mouse scurry, even through the steady patter of rain. One small step at a time, and he was at the side of the building, not wanting to enter through the hole the creatures had left in the front. They would expect that. The side door was the one O'Malley used to take his smoke breaks, and the delivery drivers used to drop off supplies. Henry eased the door open and he and Conner made their way inside, staying close to the wall.

Overhead lights flickered and sparks popped from exposed wires. The creatures had done their share of damage in the shop. Racks lay scattered across the floor, their contents broken and flung around them. Butcher paper hung from one of the light fixtures, waving at Henry and Conner as they made their way through the building. Sweat dripped from Henry's forehead into his eyes, blurring his vision. He wiped his hand across his face and continued toward the freezer door as Conner headed for the office. A horrible stench assaulted their nostrils, smelling both of old blood and new. And, above all else, the smell of the creature Henry had killed.

"Henry," Conner whispered, "Help me out here, I can't get the door open."

Henry walked over to the closed door of Richard O'Malley's office. They both leaned against it while Conner turned the handle. The door opened a few inches, then stopped. Something heavy on the other side blocked it from opening, and a horrible stench wafted out through the crack, hitting them like a fist to the face. Henry and Conner looked at each other, and they knew. They had smelled the same thing all day.

The smell of death.

Conner leaned into the door and it opened further with a sliding whoosh as it pushed away whatever had been in its path. They squeezed through the narrow opening and into the office. Henry was the last to go through, and when he closed the door behind him, he looked up to see Conner staring at the floor. In front of them, and partially blocking the door, lay the body of Victoria Perez. Still in one piece, at least, though her shoulder was sliced up as if it had gone through the meat grinder. Her eyes were closed. Conner dropped to the floor and put his fingers on her wrist, eyes locked on her chest for any sign of life, however small. A heartbeat. Slight and faltering, but there. With the amount of blood around her, it was surprising there would be any left in her body to pump.

Conner touched her face and leaned in, whispering. "Can you hear me?"

Victoria moaned in response. As her eyes fluttered open, panic set in and she pushed away from the men.

"Hey, hey, it's ok. It's us. What happened?" Henry whispered.

"... hit me... ran... hid here... locked... door," Victoria mumbled, weak and still bleeding. Her eyes closed once more.

"Ok, ok. We're gonna get you to the hospital." Henry put his arms under hers and looked at Conner. "Grab her feet, let's get her out of here."

Conner had his hand on Victoria's wrist. He leaned forward and lifted her eyelid to check for any sign of activity. Nothing. Conner slumped back to the floor, slipping her hand out of his grasp and back onto the cold tile.

"Henry."

"Conner, come on! Grab her feet!"

"Henry."

"What?"

"She's gone."

A scrape sounded from the other side of the shop, something heavy and metallic being pushed across the floor.

The men stared at each other and froze.

Henry grabbed his rifle and gestured for Conner to follow him with a finger raised to his lips. They crept back through the office door and out into the dark cool interior of the butcher shop, toward the sound. As they turned the corner to the hallway that would lead them to the walk-in freezer, several small, dark objects lay scattered around the floor in front of them. Henry poked at one of them with his foot. It was soft and yielded to his touch. He bent down to inspect it as the lights above flickered. Reaching out his hand, he recoiled the moment he made contact. One of Victoria's men. Wet, soft, and still warm. Henry stood up, covering his mouth with the back of his other hand as he attempted to contain the contents of his stomach. As they rounded another corner toward the walk-in freezer, a sea of pig and cow carcasses greeted them, covering the floor with their cold flesh.

Henry paused and took a deep breath, trying to calm the drumming of his heart against his rib cage. The heavy freezer door had been torn from its hinges, barely hanging on by a corner as it sat angled away from the opening. The door frame bulged inward. Stronger than the doors on the homes they had passed, the metal frame held, but had bent and stretched. Darkness crept out from the hole where the door had been, and a low, muffled whimper came from the other side. Neither of the men wanted to enter that black space, but the light switch sat just inside the door on the left. Henry motioned to Conner that he would flip the light when they were ready.

Inhuman panting and moaning came from within the freezer.

"On three." Henry mouthed.

Conner nodded, walked around Henry to the opposite side of the massive metallic door frame, raised his gun, and watched as Henry counted down.

Henry charged through the door with his pistol ready and Conner flipped the light. Two enormous creatures filled the freezer. Almost exactly like the animal Henry had shot, there were but a few differences. Dark red hair covered one of them, while the other was tan. Thick brow ridges jutted above their eyes, and their massive chests bowed outward. The biggest difference between them and the dead creature was that these two were enormous. The larger of the two sat crouched, unable to stand upright, and its thick red back jostled the empty hooks dangling from the ceiling. Broad shoulders, at least five feet across, hunched, trying to fit into the room as best as it could. The second animal sat on the floor of the cold space, its long tan shaggy arms swaddling the lifeless body of the creature Henry had killed just one day prior. Not as wide as the first, the second was still large enough to hold the dead animal in its arms and lap with room to spare.

Beneath the crouched red creature lay Kate. *Alive.*

A massive red hand the size of a car tire swatted toward them from the right side of the door. Henry lunged to his left and somersaulted into a firing position, facing the creature. Conner was not as agile, and the giant hand closed around his upper body. Conner screamed as the Bigfoot squeezed him.

"*Shoot* the motherfucker!" Conner screamed.

"I can't get a shot, I'll hit you!"

Henry swiveled his weapon toward the ceiling and fired at the two fluorescent lights. As the round contacted the first light, a shatter of glass and sparks rained down on them. The red creature leaped away from Henry, still grasping Conner with one hand. Conner's eyes bulged, and he was gasping for breath as the large hand squeezed him like a kid trying to pop a balloon. Henry sprinted back through the opening and into the shop, crouch-running toward the metal counter and flinging himself behind it.

What he thought he knew about the world, and what he had just faced, were two very different things. Confused, he knew for certain only this: the Bigfoot were intelligent, using Conner as a human shield like they did, and they were *enormous.*

"Get it together, Miller," Henry whispered.

He pressed the magazine release and checked his ammo count. With only eight rounds left, he swapped out his magazine for a full one. He also still had a full ten-round magazine for his rifle. He knew what to do but wasn't sure it would work. He had to try. If not for Conner, then for Kate, who was still very much alive. Henry ran back through the side entrance of the building they had come through and made his way across the street toward a metal dumpster. He slipped behind it and holstered his pistol, took the rifle that was slung across his back, and laid down in a prone position, aiming the rifle at the gaping hole in the front of the building. Reaching to the rear and not taking his eyes off the hole, he pulled the eight-round magazine from his pocket and eased the rounds out with his thumb, then placed the rounds back in his pocket. He stood, pulled back his arm as far as he could, and launched the empty magazine into the street. It flew a good fifteen yards before striking the asphalt road with a loud clank, then rattled as it danced along the roadway before stopping.

Henry lowered himself back into a prone position behind the dumpster and peered through his scope. The red Bigfoot, the larger of the two, ducked down and emerged through the hole in the building, walking forward on its knuckles as if it were a gorilla. Conner, still held in its grasp, struggled to free himself from the snake-like grip of the creature. Once outside, it rose to its full height and Henry froze. It had to be at least twelve feet tall. The Bigfoot Henry had killed, that everyone had been in awe of, was an infant compared to the thing standing in front of him. He took a deep breath and lined the crosshairs up with the creature's chest. Exhaling, Henry squeezed the trigger.

The red beast roared as it dropped to the asphalt. Panting and struggling to breathe, it flung Conner through the air toward the dumpster Henry was hiding behind. On impact, the metal caved in and the entire dumpster shifted, striking Henry in the face and cutting his head open above his right eye. Henry maintained his position and wiped the blood from his brow and out of his eyes. Conner lay on the opposite side of the dumpster, silent but for a slight gurgling sound. Blood trickled from the corner of Conner's mouth and he tried to push himself up to his feet.

He stared at Henry and mouthed a single word, "Help."

Henry pulled himself up to his knees, still using the dumpster for cover, and reached a hand toward his once-best friend. For a moment, everything was right between them.

The tan creature burst through the gaping hole in the front of the butcher shop, sending pieces of the building hurling through the night sky. It galloped the short distance to its red mate, lying panting on the ground and holding its massive hands against the small hole the bullet had left in its chest. The Bigfoot roared, and the light brown hair stood up on the back of its neck. Its head swiveled around, the large eyes finally landing on Conner as he lay just a few feet from Henry.

The creature galloped across the street toward the dumpster, covering the ground between them quickly. It grabbed Conner by the ankles and lifted him into the air, holding him at eye level with one hand, and gesturing at the injured creature with what sounded like an angry sob with the other. It slammed Conner on the ground with a thud, breaking both of his arms as he tried to cushion the impact. Conner screamed out in pain as tears and blood streamed down his forehead. The creature screamed in Conner's face while grabbing his other ankle. With little effort, the Bigfoot pulled his legs apart and the flesh at Conner's groin separated with an audible rip. Blood and intestines oozed from the wound and Conner screamed louder at the sight of his entrails before passing out.

From behind the dumpster, Henry watched. Unable to

help, he bit his knuckle to avoid crying out loud. He knew he could only get a few shots in before the creatures rushed him, and a few shots would not be enough to take them out.

The tan beast finished Conner fast, pulling him apart like a wishbone. It then dropped the two halves of his body and returned to the other animal. The larger, red creature's breathing had become more erratic, but it was able to stand and walk by using the second Bigfoot's arm for leverage. Assisting each other in a very human fashion, they entered back through the massive hole in the front of the building.

Henry moved closer to the shop to assess the situation further, knowing that Kate was still inside. He knew she wasn't dead because he could hear her labored breathing along with occasional screams of agony. Almost as if she were... in labor. Henry re-slung the rifle and took his pistol from its holster.

Kate cried out from within the freezer, "No, don't take him!"

16

Henry ran through the front opening of the shop with his pistol at the ready and headed toward the freezer. The first creature he saw was the tan one that had murdered Conner. Henry fired his weapon as fast as he could pull the trigger, striking the Bigfoot in the legs and abdomen as it roared in anger and pain, dropping to its knees. With his weapon empty, Henry scanned the room for anything he could use and noticed the metal hooks hanging from the ceiling of the freezer. Henry leaped into the air and twisted, throwing his shoulders deep into the tan fur on the animal's chest. It fell into the meat hook and the sharp point pierced the back of the creature, just below its shoulder. It writhed in pain, struggling to free itself. The larger, red creature moved toward its impaled mate, but the tan animal raised its hands in protest and bellowed in a strange language. The red Bigfoot stopped and turned to face Henry. It was holding a small bloody object in its massive hand. It had Kate's baby, still covered in blood from the delivery, and wailing. Henry looked down at the creature's feet and saw Kate laying on the floor with a growing red pool between her blood-soaked thighs. Her eyes fluttered closed and she panted, her face pale and covered in sweat. The beast lifted the baby to its face and stared at it, before sniffing the baby and contorting its mouth into what looked like a smile.

Frozen with fear and panic, Henry's eyes widened as the red creature grabbed Kate with its free hand and hurled her at the door. Her body stopped in mid-air, jerking as blood spurted and dripped from her chest. Kate, impaled on a hook, rocked back and forth as if she were a human pendulum. Henry stared at the body of the love of his life and what he had, until recently, thought was the mother of his child. He never noticed the tan Bigfoot free itself from its own hook, or the large arm swinging toward him.

With another roar, the massive creature lunged forward. He yanked Henry into the air and flung him through the door of the freezer and into the shop, his body coming to rest in a crumpled heap in front of the cash register. Henry groaned in pain and tried to crawl behind the counter, but the animal was too fast. Large hands encircled both of Henry's ankles and jerked backward, bringing him back out into the open. He could smell its putrid breath as it leaned down, inches from his face. Tears rolled down the creature's cheeks as it stared at him.

One giant palm wrapped around his body and another grabbed his arm. After seeing what happened to Conner, Henry knew what was coming. He wrestled the pistol from its holster and swung it around into the animal's face. Four quick shots fired, the muzzle flashing with each shot before the creature knocked it out of Henry's grasp. Before the gun could hit the floor, the animal had returned its hand to Henry's arm and squeezed. With a jerk, Henry's arm popped off. Blinded by the searing pain, the shop wavered in front of him, and lights danced in his eyes as if he were staring into the sun.

With a cold spasm creeping across his chest, Henry's pain faded, and he watched the somber creatures crawl out of the shop. Once past the door, the Bigfoot stretched to their full height and ran past Kellen out into the storm, and toward the mountains. One clutching their dead child, and the other holding Kate's newborn son. Henry's heart echoed the pounding of their heavy feet on the pavement, until they reached the tree line and everything went quiet.

17

Kellen Tsosie stood at the edge of the clearing, shielding his eyes from the rising sun with one hand while holding the other across his chest as a sign of respect. He knew it would take years to rebuild the trust between his people and the clan. A trust broken by a rebellious tribal son who had gone too far from the safe zone and a good man who made a mistake. But it could happen, the alliance was holding for the moment, however shaky. His presence there proved at least that much. Terrified at first to go, he knew there could be no other way to move forward than to make the trek to the foothills of Mt. Jarvis.

In the center of the clearing, on a mat of intertwined pine and hemlock twigs, lay the creature Henry Miller had killed, bent into a fetal position with his hands and feet tied together. His parents, the two beasts that had torn through the town of Easton Falls, stood in front of their child's corpse. A paste of volcanic ash and water covered the thick fur on their faces, gray remnants still visible on their hands as they held their arms across their chest and bowed their heads.

While Kellen's presence was expected, he knew enough not to push it too far after everything that had happened. He stayed close to the tree line, out of earshot but still in view of the elaborate burial ceremony coming to a close in front of him. The parents of the dead creature placed a cloth over their child, then marked a circle on it with the volcanic ash paste. Four other beasts emerged from the shadows, all as enormous as the first two, ready to carry the child to his final resting place. The parents stepped into line behind the four holding the covered body, and they shuffled toward the base of Mt. Jarvis, shoulders slumped and hearts heavy.

The group stopped at a grave, dug earlier by another member of the clan the moment they had returned home. The four creatures placed the covered corpse into the grave and proceeded to lay large gray and white rocks on top of him. As the last part of the cloth was covered, a deep, guttural wail came from both parents. It echoed off the mountainside and into the forest around them, reaching Kellen. A tear tracked down his face, mourning not only for the creature beneath the rocks but for everyone who had died along the way. And for what? A wandering child and an accidental shooting? He sighed, knowing he would have an even bigger mess to clean up once he returned to town, and unsure how to spin any of it to protect the identity of the clan in front of him.

At the close of the ritual, the dead creature's father turned to face Kellen. He held his right arm up in a sign of peace, crossing the distance between them not only that day but for the days to come. Kellen raised his right arm in return and turned to go. Behind him, the rest of the clan emerged from the shadows. Thousands lifted their faces to the sky and wailed, echoing the parents of the slain beast.

SEATTLE TIMES

Tuesday, September 17th, 2007

Easton Falls Survivor

Robert Williams, one of the survivors of the Easton Falls Massacre, has a lot to say about the events that unfolded last Sunday, September 15th. Although found locked in a prison cell in the Easton Falls Police Department building early Monday morning, Robert insists he placed himself there as a measure of protection. Williams claims the full blame for the massacre falls on the shoulders of Henry Miller, aged 36, of Easton Falls, Washington. Miller, according to Williams, set a 'Bigfoot loose on the city'. Attempts to reach Miller for comment have failed, and he is currently in the care of Chambers Memorial Hospital. Authorities are not looking into the matter of a Bigfoot any further, as it is clear Williams is suffering from Post-Traumatic Stress Disorder, and, due to the amount of alcohol found in his bloodstream, his account cannot be verified or taken seriously.

SEATTLE TIMES

Wednesday, September 18th, 2007

In Memoriam

The Seattle Times staff would like to express our sincere condolences to the family and friends of our sister press, The Easton Falls Times, in Easton Falls, Washington. While a few reporters are still missing, the rest of the staff have been confirmed deceased after the deadly bear attacks in Easton Falls last Sunday, September 15th. This has been an extreme blow to the heart and soul of our two presses, and we remain committed to honoring their memories by covering this attack in the best way we know how, through the press. Rest in peace, brothers and sisters. You are not forgotten.

EXPOSED!

Saturday, August 9th, 2013

The "Wild Boy" Of Easton Falls

Multiple reports of a "wild boy" have emerged recently from the Easton Falls, Washington, area, as developers have broken ground at the edges of the Black Forest. The developers, Fidelity Builders, are the first sign that Easton Falls, famously known for the Massacre that occurred in September of 2007, has begun to bounce back from the horrendous and costly event six years prior.

Frances Lyons and Pauline Rogers claim they encountered the 'wild boy' last summer when they were camping near the southern gully of the Black Forest. They were sitting in front of their campfire one morning when a small boy with curly brown hair and blue eyes appeared at the edge of their clearing. Naked and wild-eyed, they were at first concerned for the safety of the boy and said they had assumed he was lost. But when Lyons approached him, he seemed to speak in an unfamiliar language, then turned and ran into the forest. They did not encounter him again for the remainder of their trip.

This past June, Billy Bardeaux claims he saw the same boy while hunting in the area, and authorities took the claims seriously enough to comb the forests in search of this 'wild boy'. Unfortunately, the search came up empty-handed as a large tree had fallen, blocking the only path into that part of the forest. They said they may resume the search once the tree is cleared, but are not positive at this time.

ACKNOWLEDGMENTS

Thank you to Dad (Carl Mikel, Sr.). You have always believed, both in us and in Bigfoot. To Linda Mikel Hartsfield, Rhonda Cantu, Heather Lander, Andrea Goyan, and Laurie Hicks: thank you for your wonderful beta reading skills, tips, and suggestions. To James Karm and Jim Sybers, glad we made it home. To those who didn't, you are never forgotten.

ABOUT THE AUTHORS

Holly Rae Garcia is a photographer and author. She lives on the Texas Coast with her family and five large dogs.

www.HollyRaeGarcia.com.
Twitter @HollyRaeGarcia
Instagram@HollyRaeGarcia

Ryan Prentice Garcia is a safety manager, US Army veteran, and author. Raised all over the world as an Army brat, he made the Texas Coast his home.

www.RyanPrenticeGarcia.com
Twitter@PrenticeGarcia
Instagram@Prentice2525

Holly and **Ryan** have been married since 2015.

ALSO BY HOLLY RAE GARCIA

Come Join the Murder

Printed in Great Britain
by Amazon

62883189R00080